BLINDSIDED

A TITANIUM SECURITY CHRISTMAS NOVELLA

NEW YORK TIMES AND *USA TODAY* BESTSELLING AUTHOR

KAYLEA
CROSS

BLINDSIDED: A TITANIUM SECURITY CHRISTMAS NOVELLA

Dedication

This one goes out to all my Titanium readers. It's been a long time since I hung out with the team, and I so enjoyed catching up with all the couples.

It might be Christmastime, but this story is the opposite of light and fluffy. Buckle your seatbelts, gang!

Author's Note

Dear readers,

I've always wanted to pen a Christmas novella, and writing about the Titanium crew gave me a chance to do just that, while getting to hang out with my old buddies again.

It wouldn't be a romantic suspense story without a few hair-raising and emotionally wrenching scenes, so get ready to ride this rollercoaster of highs and lows along with the characters.

Love, friends and family are what make the holidays such a special time, and the Titanium crew is going to realize that more than ever within these pages. I hope you enjoy this one.

Happy reading!

Kaylea Cross

CHAPTER ONE

Alex Rycroft fiddled with his right cufflink a second longer before leaving the master bedroom and heading for the stairs with the sound of the vacuum humming in his ears. Grace was downstairs somewhere, cleaning the hell out of the place for the second time in three days. It didn't matter that he'd threatened to throw the damn thing into the lake and every cleaning supply they owned if she didn't slow down, the stubborn woman never listened.

And she'd just go buy new ones if he did.

Leave me alone, I'm nesting. This place is my home and my castle now, and I want it to look its best when everyone gets here tomorrow, she'd told him before he'd hit the shower ten minutes ago. They were expecting the entire Titanium crew for a reunion of sorts, which included an early Christmas dinner.

He knew how much Grace loved this place, and that she needed an outlet to keep her busy now that she was wrapping up the last of her consulting jobs. Since he was getting close to retirement they'd been looking for a place here in upstate New York to relocate to, and the moment she'd seen this grand old lady of a Victorian perched on a hill at the end of quiet street overlooking the lake, it had been all over. He might as well have whipped out his checkbook right then and there on the front porch.

As he reached the doorway to his office, he paused, the familiar stress creeping over him that he should still be working right now. At the moment he had over a dozen priority cases going on. He'd done what he could on them today, knowing he'd be unable to work over the next couple of days. The workaholic in him wanted to squeeze in just a few more minutes on them, but he kept walking, his dress shoes silent on the thick hall runner.

The house was over a hundred years old, and had needed some work, including having all the carpets ripped out and the antique wood floors refinished. For the past several months he'd watched a large chunk of their savings get eaten away on renovations, but Grace was so damn excited and caught up in nesting mode, he didn't even care about the money.

Until last December, they'd had a vacation place right on the ski hill in Lake Placid. Then it had been attacked.

He and Zahra, a cryptologist he'd recruited years ago and the closest thing he'd ever had to a daughter, had gone up there to meet Matt DeLuca—the commander of the FBI's Hostage Rescue Team—and DeLuca's now wife, Briar, after her life had been threatened. The people targeting her had somehow tracked her there and mounted an attack, and Briar had barely escaped with her life.

After that incident, his and Grace's winter vacation home hadn't felt so cozy and safe anymore. Because he was a paranoid bastard, he'd put it up for sale immediately. All for the best, and he liked this house way better anyhow. It had plenty of extra bedrooms for when they had company, and he'd had a top of the line security system installed by a couple of the Titanium Security guys before they'd moved in.

The afternoon light was already fading as he passed the small oval window set into the wall beside the main staircase. Fat snowflakes drifted past the leaded-glass pane. They were due for a good six inches up here tonight, and a dusting in New York City. The roads were going to be slick. He'd better get a move on if he didn't want to be late.

Downstairs on the main floor, the sound of the vacuum grew even louder. Walking past the new, gourmet kitchen, he found Grace in the adjoining living room, vacuuming the hell out of the area carpet in front of the fireplace. Dr. Grace Fallon-Rycroft, chemical engineer and chem weapons expert for the U.N.

Her brain was the sexiest thing about her, and that was saying a *lot* because the woman could get him raging hot with a single look from those pretty aqua eyes.

She stopped when she saw him, straightening with a smile that looked a little weary as she switched the power button off. "Hey."

"You're going to wear out that carpet if you don't stop soon," he told her.

She pushed a strand of auburn hair out of her face and cracked a grin. "Just wanted to do one more cleaning before tomorrow."

"The house is already perfect."

Every inch of the place was as spotless as it had been yesterday, and looked like something out of a magazine spread. He'd wanted to hire a cleaning service but Grace had refused, wanting to do it all herself. She'd put flannel sheets and Christmas-themed patchwork quilts on all the beds this morning, and adorned each room with little ornaments and a small, decorated tree.

She'd also baked God only knew how many varieties of cookies and other treats over the past two days. The chest freezer in the garage was jammed full, and the turkey was already brining in a cooler beside it.

Now he just wanted his wife to freaking *rest*. He'd run dozens of errands over the past two days to try and take the bulk of the work off her shoulders, and still she refused to slow down. There were faint shadows beneath her eyes. He didn't want to see them get any darker.

Alex closed the distance between them and wrapped his arms around her waist from behind, nuzzling the back of her neck, then the side. On the spot that always made her melt and shiver, and she didn't disappoint him now. "I'm way more worried about you wearing out than the carpet."

"You worry too much. I'm fine, and I already had a nap earlier."

"For all of twenty minutes." He slid his hands beneath the bottom of her pink cashmere sweater to caress the tender skin of her abdomen, his fingertips lingering over the scars there. Her biggest regret was that the emergency hysterectomy had taken away the chance for her to have a baby after the attack in Mombasa, Kenya. It killed him that he hadn't been there to protect her that night.

"I'm way too wired to sleep right now." She turned in his arms and lifted up onto her toes to brush a kiss over his lips. "You look good enough to eat, by the way." She leaned in to press her nose against the side of his neck and inhale deeply. "Mmm, and you smell delicious too."

Instantly a surge of blood rushed to his groin, making his already snug tux pants downright uncomfortable. He tightened his arms around her and nuzzled her jaw. "Makes me wish I was staying home with you tonight instead of going to this gala."

She made a soft sound of sympathy. "I'll make it up to you when you get home."

"Yeah?" That sounded interesting. Grace had a vivid and erotic imagination when she wanted to.

"Yeah." She kissed him again, her lips lingering on his this time.

Because he was contemplating lying her down in front of the fireplace and peeling her clothes off right now, he broke the kiss and reined in his libido as he gazed down at her. "So, everything still a go for tonight?"

"Just waiting for the call." Her eyes sparkled up at him, filled with anticipation. "I can't wait."

He grinned, her excitement infectious. She'd been looking forward to tomorrow's festivities even more since they'd begun planning the surprise with Zahra a few weeks ago.

"Promise me you'll stop cleaning and put your feet up for a while," he murmured. There were big changes headed their way in the next few weeks, and she was going to need all the energy she could muster. For the most part she'd recovered completely from the sarin gas exposure two years ago that could easily have killed her, but she still suffered frequent headaches and got tired easily.

"I will, right after I prep a few last minute things in the kitchen."

He frowned, disliking that plan. "I thought we took care of all that already, and that Claire is bringing the rest tomorrow?"

"We did, and she is. I just have a couple things left I want to do. No big deal."

He could tell her to rest until he was blue in the face, but it wouldn't change the outcome. When she put her mind to something, Grace was a petite steamroller, and he'd learned to simply get the hell out of her way.

"Snow's started, and the traffic's gonna be insane getting into the city, so I'd better go." He hated leaving her though. There would always be a part of him that was terrified something or someone might take her away from him. Just one of the ghosts from his past he'd learned to live with.

The happiness in her eyes dimmed. "Sorry I'm not going with you."

"Don't be, it's fine, and it'll probably be boring as hell anyway."

Ever since the attack in Kenya, she was uneasy

at galas or any events with a large crowd, and he didn't blame her. He was just grateful that this strong, independent and incredible woman had come back into his life, because for a long time he'd been certain he'd lost her forever. He'd promised Hunter and Khalia he'd be at the gala tonight, and Grace had other things to take care of.

A familiar ring tone broke the quiet. Zahra. Grace pulled her phone from her pocket and answered. "Hey, Zahr. Did they call you yet?" She met Alex's gaze, and smiled, the laugh lines at the corner of her eyes standing out. She hated them but he adored every line on her face. "Perfect. I'll text you later. Bye."

Sounded like everything was going according to plan so far. "Well?"

"It's a go. He's on the plane right now, and I pick him up at twenty after seven." Her eyes sparkled in the twinkling lights of the Christmas tree they'd put up in the corner of the room. The same one they'd decorated at their place in Lake Placid. He'd proposed to her next to it.

"You be careful driving in this snow." He'd had snow tires put on her vehicle last week. Where Grace's safety was concerned, he took no chances.

"I will." She kissed him again, then pushed him toward the door. "Drive safe and text me when you get there so I don't worry."

He stopped and curved a hand around her nape, stared down into her eyes. "Love you, angel."

"Love you back."

Unable to resist the temptation, he dipped down to kiss those soft lips once more. "I'd tell you not to wait up for me, but you will anyway, won't you?"

A gentle smile. "You know me so well."

He grunted. "Yeah."

He'd no sooner shut and locked the front door behind him than the vacuum started up again. Shaking his head, he hit the remote starter and headed for his SUV parked in the driveway.

****

When he'd planned this the other day, he hadn't expected to feel any different now than he had then, but he did. He felt complete in a way he hadn't before, and more at peace than he'd ever thought possible.

Clasping Khalia's hand tight in his own, Hunter held the heavy wooden door open for her and guided her out into the chilly afternoon air. The moment they left the building, the constant motion of New York City surrounded them with its noise and energy.

On the street before them traffic was busy as always in uptown Manhattan, the honks of horns and distant sirens filling the air. Overhead the sky was a deep leaden gray, a light snow flurry falling, the air cold enough to turn their breath into vapor.

The cold couldn't touch him though. Not today, and never with her beside him.

"Oh, look, it's snowing," Khalia breathed, and paused on the top step to close her eyes and tip her face up to the sky.

She was so fucking beautiful she almost hurt his eyes.

Her long, dark, curly hair was pinned into an elaborate up-do for tonight's gala, and the ruby-red satin gown she wore made her skin glow. Tiny snowflakes gathered on her cheeks as she stood there, dropping on her nose and lashes, settling into the curve of her glossy red smile.

A sudden wave of territorial hunger swept over him. Hunter gathered her into his arms and bent to take that sultry mouth, the icy flakes melting beneath the stroke of his lips and tongue. She made a purring sound and wound her arms around his neck, leaning fully into him, the feel of her breasts pressed against his chest driving him crazy.

When he lifted his head a minute later her pale green eyes were heavy-lidded and her cheeks were flushed. "Cold?" he murmured.

"Not even a little. I'm just happy. Really happy."

He smiled. "Me too. No regrets?"

She shook her head. "None. Except that it's going to be a few hours until we can get to our hotel."

Catching her hand again, he led her down the steps, toward the limo waiting for them at the curb. "We'll improvise."

The driver popped out and rushed around to open the back door for them. Hunter helped her into the backseat, getting an eyeful of creamy cleavage as she bent over in that gorgeous gown and slid across the wide leather seat. "We've got an hour to kill before we need to be at the gala," he said to the driver. The sun was already setting, and it would be dark soon. "Can you drive us around so we can look at the Christmas lights?"

"Of course, sir."

Hunter shut the door and immediately hit the switch to raise the divider between the driver and the back of the limo.

"You really want to take a tour of the Christmas lights right now?" Khalia asked him, sounding surprised.

"Nope," he said, already undoing his bowtie and taking off his jacket. He wasn't interested in a damn thing right now except the woman in front of him.

Tossing the jacket aside, he pulled her into his lap, positioning her so that her bottom snuggled up against his erection. "And if I do this right, the only lights you'll be seeing are the fireworks on the backs of your eyelids when I make you come."

"Oh, I can't wait to go on *that* tour," she said with a seductive laugh, and cupped the side of his face to bring his mouth to hers.

Hunter started to slide his left hand into her hair, his gaze catching on his wedding band. Titanium, of course. Khalia made a sound of protest and pulled his hand away. "Don't muss me up. The stylist worked for an hour to get my hair like this," she whispered against his mouth with a little smile before resuming the kiss.

He wanted to do a hell of a lot more than just muss her up, but they were the founders and co-chairs of Scottie's Foundation, and in just over an hour they'd both have to be up on stage in front of almost four hundred people.

He'd make an effort to be as careful about not ruining her hair and makeup as he could stand to be, but all he wanted was to get her naked and too lost in what she was feeling to care about anything else but the need to come. He wasn't worried about the driver lowering the divider. Hunter had already tipped him well and made it clear he wanted privacy.

Nipping at her lower lip, he reached back to find the zipper at the bottom of her shoulder blades and tugged hard.

Something popped.

She squealed against his mouth and pushed away. "No, don't tear it. Here, let me." She sat up and reached behind her for the top of the zipper.

Her eyes held a wicked, sultry glow that made him even harder as she knelt there on the leather seat and slowly drew down the top of the strapless gown. His gaze locked on the sexy-as-fuck black lace push-up bra she wore beneath it, molding to her breasts and lifting them up so they practically spilled out of the cups.

With a final tug on the zipper she undid it all the way to her waist, then came up on her knees to shimmy out of it, revealing the tiny, matching black thong she wore. A low, possessive growl vibrated deep in his chest at the sight of her.

Unable to stand it a second longer he reached for her, settling his hands on the curve of her hips as he dragged her back into his body. Her lips parted to the stroke of his tongue as he delved inside to taste her, tease her, her fingers already undoing the buttons of his dress shirt.

He skimmed the shape of her body with his palms, cupped her breasts through the bra while he licked and nipped his way over her jaw and down the side of her neck until he could bury his face in her cleavage. She hummed in approval and rocked her hips against him, spreading his shirt wide so she could run her hands over his chest and shoulders. It was a huge turn-on to know his body aroused her.

With one impatient tug he undid the front catch on the bra, and her breasts spilled into his waiting hands. He groaned at the feel of her lush flesh filling his palms, swept his thumbs over the hard, dusky peaks as he nuzzled her softness. Khalia gasped and speared her fingers into his hair, pulling him closer. Demanding more.

"Don't muss me up," he teased, and her answering laugh dissolved into a soft moan of pleasure as he parted his lips and took one straining nipple into his mouth.

The scent of her perfume mixed with the sweeter scent of his skin. He was lost, already drunk on her by the time she had his tux pants undone and curled both hands around the hot, rigid flesh of his erection. He shuddered at her sure grip and pushed into her hands, desperate for her touch. For the relief only she could give him.

Pushing the dress the rest of the way off her, he wrapped an arm around her hips and pulled her astride his lap, splaying his hand across her ass to press her tight to his aching cock. She made a murmuring sound and widened her stance, holding his face to her breasts while he sucked and she rubbed her center against his erection.

"You make me so wet," she whimpered, bending to curve her upper body around him, her mouth teasing a spot just below his ear.

Good, and he was going to make her wetter yet.

Switching to the other nipple, he cradled her breast with one hand and let the other wander over the bare curve of her rear, tracing the line of the thong as it disappeared in the crevice there. She shivered and nipped at his jaw, hungry for more.

His cock was swollen, desperate to get inside her, but it would have to wait. He was too focused on her right now, determined to make this memorable for her. Gently he stroked his fingers over the thin scrap of fabric between her cheeks, pausing to skim the sensitive skin beside it as he dipped between her legs. Her breath caught, the sexy sound right against his ear.

Sucking a little harder now, he rubbed his tongue against her captive nipple and eased his fingertips beneath the lace. The feel of her hot, slick folds made his cock jerk.

The hand in his hair tightened, her other flying to his shoulder and digging in. Each tiny moan she gave pushed the need inside him higher. She was so soft, so wet against his fingers as he stroked her, spreading the evidence of her arousal up to her clit where he swirled a tender circle.

"Oh, Hunter, yeah," she breathed, and let her head fall back.

He released her nipple long enough to shift his gaze upward and drink in the sight of her like that. Eyes closed as she leaned back, glossy red lips parted, those delectable breasts and their tight peaks inches from his face while she rocked against his hand. Lost in the moment and the pleasure he was giving her.

The dark, possessive hunger he felt for her surged to the surface. He released her breast and cupped her nape instead, drawing her down into a deep, desperate kiss. She moaned into his mouth and reached down to push at her panties, wriggling out of them while he shoved his pants down his thighs.

This time when she settled over him, his cock met warm, sultry flesh. His entire body tightened and he shifted his free hand around between them to stroke at the hard bud of her clit.

Khalia shivered and gasped into his mouth, then gripped the base of his cock with her fist and positioned him against her folds. Tongue twining with his, the urgency burning hot and bright between them, she slowly sank down on him.

Sensation blasted up his spine. Her heat surrounded him, engulfing and squeezing until his heart pounded and he could barely breathe. Then she began to ride him in a slow, sensual rhythm and he almost lost it then and there.

Fighting through the haze of acute pleasure, he focused on kissing her and continued to stroke her most sensitive spot with a slick fingertip. Soft. Gentle. Just the way she liked it, letting her pleasure build while she set the pace, sinking up and down in a sensual, fluid rhythm.

He knew the exact moment when her orgasm began to build. She broke the kiss and pressed her forehead to his, a plaintive moan spilling from her lips. Her pussy clenched around him, milking him like a greedy fist.

Hunter gripped her around the hips with one arm

and slid forward to set one knee on the floor. Her eyes fluttered open in confusion but he was already swinging her up and around, laying her lengthwise on the long leather seat. He stared at her for a moment, stroking a curly tendril away from her flushed cheek.

She gazed up at him with passion-glazed eyes, her breasts moving with each erratic breath. Her lips were swollen from his kisses, her nipples hard from his mouth, and the beautiful ruby satin dress crumpled around her. Her pale skin glowed in the lights from the city coming in through the tinted windows, naked except for the pair of spiked black heels strapped around her ankles.

The image of her like this was already seared into his brain forever.

With a soft growl he moved between her open thighs, gripping the backs to fold her legs up against her body. She set those sexy heels onto his shoulders, her eyes darkening with longing and need, and gripped his shoulders to pull him close.

He took that lush mouth, plunged his tongue inside as he reached down to caress her clit. Within moments she was mewling and writhing beneath him, and he couldn't wait a moment longer.

Pressing the head of his cock against her, he broke the kiss and stared down into her face as he surged forward, burying himself in her heat. Her eyes squeezed shut and her head tipped back on the leather, a fierce cry of satisfaction tearing from her.

Hunter took her hard and fast, knowing she was close, unable to slow down now. She was his now, and nobody would ever take her from him. He wanted the whole fucking world to know it.

As he plunged deep again she contracted around his cock and let out a sob of pleasure as she began to come. He shut his eyes and drove harder, deeper, unable to get enough of her.

Through the fire racing up his spine he felt her arms wrap around his neck. Sliding his hand from between them, he seized her hips and relentlessly went after his own release. Five more strokes and it blasted through him, sheeting his vision white and pulling every muscle in his body tight.

Chest heaving, suddenly weak all over, he released her hips and collapsed onto his forearms above her, his face resting in the curve of her neck. She wiggled and he lifted up enough to help her slide her legs off his shoulders.

Immediately she wrapped them around his thighs, her contented sigh cooling the damp skin at his temple. Her hands wandered over his naked back and shoulders, her touch gentle, lips soft as an angel's wings as she brushed kisses over the side of his sweaty face. "So, how's my hair?" she whispered.

He laughed against her soft skin. "Perfect."

"You didn't even look."

"Don't need to. I know you're still perfect."

Her fingertips whispered over his shoulders. "I love you so much."

The whispered words laid his heart wide open.

Even after all this time he still didn't know if he even deserved her. She was high class and wickedly smart; he was blue collar all the way, a man who'd spent most of his adult life earning his living from his skills with a weapon. Somehow she didn't mind all that, even though he knew she worried about him when he was on a job.

All he knew was that she was the best thing in his life. She'd done so much for him. She'd been there for him at every turn since they'd gotten together, supporting his ambition to one day be the sole owner of Titanium Security, and doing the lion's share of the work in getting Scottie's Foundation up and running. In the past eighteen months she'd almost single-handedly turned it into one of the fastest growing charities in the U.S.

He'd be lost without her. "I love you too," he whispered back.

Before the night was out, he was going to show her exactly how much.

CHAPTER TWO

Z ahra paused in the middle of putting on mascara when her phone buzzed on the vanity with a new text message from Grace.

On my way to the airport. Will send you a picture once I pick him up. Alex should be there soon. Enjoy the gala.

She smiled. *Awesome, thanks. Drive safe.*

She was lucky to have them in her life. Her own father was currently serving a life sentence for murdering her mother and almost killing her. Alex was her boss, but he'd been more of a father to her these past years than her real one ever had, and for that he would always have her undying love and loyalty. She loved Grace too. They'd all planned this surprise so carefully, and now they were down to the last few hours.

Zahra couldn't wait. She didn't want anything to go wrong now, or for Sean to get suspicious that something was up.

Picking up the tube of mascara again, she looked at herself in the mirror. Normally she didn't wear much, if any makeup, but tonight was a special night for the Titanium family and she wanted to look her best. And there was also a part of her that was hoping to wow her husband out of the funk he'd fallen into recently. She'd splurged on the emerald green, floor-length gown a month ago, imagining the look on Sean's face when he saw her in it.

Butterflies swirled in the pit of her stomach, a mix of excitement and nerves as she swept her long, dark hair up and secured it with a clip at the back of her head then pulled little tendrils out around her face to frame it. The plan she'd been concocting over the past few weeks *had* to work. She refused to watch her husband slip away from her and do nothing to stop it.

Exiting the steamy bathroom, she glanced around the hotel suite she'd booked for them, but Sean wasn't on the bed or the couch watching TV. She found him in the adjoining sitting room, sitting on the window bench, staring out at the brightly lit skyline of Manhattan. He was already dressed in his tux, his jacket hanging from the top of his cane, which was propped up against the sill.

Her heart twisted at the sight of him sitting like that.

He'd been through so much since they'd met, and he wasn't even close to the same man he'd been back then. The lighthearted, often sarcastic prankster she'd fallen in love with was barely recognizable anymore. There were glimpses of the old Sean, but they were getting rarer and rarer.

Seeing that hurt far more than the way he'd been pulling away from her recently.

Suffering such devastating injuries to his legs

had been as hard on his mind as it had his body. It didn't matter that he realized how lucky he was to still have both his legs, and was able to walk again.

Somewhere along the long road to where they were now, he'd lost his zest for life. He still worked fulltime for Titanium, mostly tech stuff and logistics, but the permanency of his disability had finally hit home, along with the knowledge that he would only ever be able to work from behind a desk for the rest of his career.

She pushed away from the doorframe and started toward him, the heels of her shoes sinking into the plush carpet. A twinge of pain shot through her right hip. She'd slipped on any icy patch on the sidewalk yesterday, exacerbating the pain in her bad hip. The muscles pulled with every step but she ignored it. "See anything interesting down there?"

He turned his head, his dark gaze locking on her, then sliding down the length of her body and back up. A spark of hope burned inside her at the sudden heat in his eyes and the grin tugging at his mouth. "Wow, look at you."

She couldn't help but smile. "You like?"

He circled a finger in the air. "Turn around, let me see from the back too."

Zahra turned in as graceful a circle as she could, given her bad hip and the four inch heels she had on. High heels were a killer for her leg, let alone such high ones, but this dress demanded them. Tonight she wanted to be a walking sex goddess, so a little more pain than usual for a few hours wasn't that high a price to pay.

"Well?" she asked, stopping to face him again.

"You look so damn sexy, sweetness," he said, the way his voice dropped an octave making her insides flutter. "Even New York City all decked out for the holidays can't hold a candle to you."

She flushed at the compliment, secretly touched. She'd been starting to worry he wasn't attracted to her anymore. "Thank you. You don't look too bad yourself." On their first official date he'd been all dressed up to take her to a different gala. He was every bit as sexy now as he had been back then.

No, more. Since then she'd seen just how strong he was as he'd fought to regain the use of his legs. She was proud of him, and even though she was frustrated that he refused to get help from a therapist, she was trying to be patient as she rode this rollercoaster with him.

He started to get up but she crossed to him before he could push off the bench and sat on it, facing him. She slipped a hand around the back of his neck, leaned forward to touch her lips to his. He made a low sound of approval in the back of his throat and wrapped his heavy arms around her, pulling her tight to his hard chest, then slanted his mouth over hers.

The unexpected show of hunger and interest from him thrilled her. It had been more than three weeks since he'd reached for her like this.

She curled her fingers into the soft hair at his nape, her other hand sliding up to grip his thick shoulder. Their sex life had suffered as he'd begun to slide emotionally over the past few weeks and she was desperately hoping that tonight would get them back on track.

Because when a gorgeous alpha male like Sean Dunphy suddenly lost interest in sex, it meant something was seriously wrong.

She eased away from him, her body aching for more, and stared into his eyes that had gone molten with desire. "We have to get going," she whispered with regret. Much as she'd love to stay and finish what they'd started here, they were cutting the timing close as it was.

He made a face but nodded. "Yeah, okay."

"It'll be fun. We'll get to see the whole gang again, and it's for a good cause."

Then tomorrow, they'd all go to Alex and Grace's new house upstate and spend a couple nights there together to celebrate an early Christmas. Where Sean's surprise would be waiting, if all went according to plan tonight. After that they'd be flying to Coeur D'Alene to spend the holidays with his family. She was counting on that to help begin pulling him out of the darkness that threatened to steal the man she loved from her.

He grunted in reply and leaned in to nip at her lower lip.

She nibbled at his mouth for a moment longer then put a hand on the side of his face and smiled at him. She still loved him, more than ever, and he loved her. And so she refused to let him lose this battle. "Just think of what you get to look forward to when we come back here later."

"Already am."

Good. Tonight was looking up already.

She stood, pausing a second when the muscles in her bad hip protested the sudden movement. He set a big hand on her other hip to steady her. "I'm okay. Just moved too fast."

She held out a hand to help him up but his jaw tightened and he pushed up on his own, refusing her help. He reached for his jacket and swung it on, then reached for the cane and paused.

Zahra held her breath and waited. He loathed the cane. Both the need for it, and because it had become a symbol of his physical limitations.

He turned away from it, his body and expression rigid as he limped toward the door. She bit back the words waiting on the tip of her tongue, an admonishment for risking further injury without the cane to support him, especially since it might be slippery out. Saying it wouldn't do any good. It certainly wouldn't change his mind, and it would definitely make him angry and sullen.

Pick your battles, Zahra.

Smothering a frustrated sigh, she grabbed her evening bag and wrap from the table on the way past and followed him. Something had to give, and if the next few days didn't start to bring the old Sean back to her, she didn't know what she was going to do.

*****

We're on our way. See you there.

Claire groaned as she read Zahra's text. To have any hope of arriving to the gala on time, they had to leave in the next minute and Gage wasn't even dressed yet.

We're leaving shortly, she responded, and prayed

23

it was true. She wasn't normally one for formal events, but she was looking forward to this gala. After losing her veteran brother to suicide because he hadn't been able to cope with the moral and emotional injuries he'd sustained while fighting overseas, she was happy to support a foundation that worked to prevent such devastating loss and suffering.

While Gage kept talking on his phone in no apparent hurry to end the conversation, Claire gestured to him to hurry the hell up then shoved a lipstick into her handbag. Balanced on one foot while she wrestled the buckle of one high heel into place around her ankle, she bent to rummage in the hotel room closet for the other.

"Yeah, we're both looking forward to seeing you too, sweetheart," Gage said to his daughter in his North Carolina drawl, stark naked as he ambled away from Claire across the room to where she'd left his tux hanging up in the garment bag in the bathroom.

He still talked a bit louder than he should at times, but his hearing would never be a hundred percent again. After having his eardrums perforated in an explosion that had almost killed him, he was lucky that hearing loss was the only permanent damage he'd suffered.

Come on, Gage, move that fine ass of yours and hurry up. She hated being late. Gage was Hunter's right-hand-man, and she didn't want to disrespect him and Khalia by showing up after the welcoming speeches started.

"We'll wait until you get there to go pick out a

tree. There's a lot about ten minutes outside of town that sells spruces, just like we used to get when you were little."

Aww, he was getting all sentimental about the upcoming visit. This Christmas was going to be extra special for him. For the first time since his divorce, Janelle was coming out to spend the holidays with them at their place in the Outer Banks, soon after they got back from Grace and Alex's.

He paused to grab his shaving kit from the vanity, his scowl visible in the mirror. "What about that guy you were seeing? You're not bringing him, are you? Not sure I could stomach looking at him across the table at Christmas dinner."

Claire shook her head at him, could just imagine how hard Janelle rolled her eyes at that one.

"Sure, she's right here. You want to say hello?" He looked over his shoulder at her.

Claire shook her head at him frantically, tapping her watch and raising her eyebrows. She loved Janelle like crazy, even if she was a moody teenager, but they seriously had to get moving. There was something about hotel rooms that added a certain spice to a vacation. They'd gotten…distracted after they'd checked in and were now running behind.

Gage grinned at her, bright blue eyes twinkling with amusement. "Actually we're just running out the door to catch a cab to the gala. She'll call you later." He disappeared into the bathroom, the deep murmur of his voice floating back to her as he kept talking to Janelle. A minute later he came out with his pants on, a white dress shirt in one fist.

He shrugged into it with a casual, masculine move, and Claire got distracted again by the sight of all those thick muscles on display, along with all those sexy tats that covered both arms and his chest.

Especially the one in the center of his chest. Every time she saw her name inked into the skin above his heart, she melted a little.

A fact he knew extremely well and used to his advantage often.

Catching her staring, he flexed his pecs, one at a time in rapid succession, making her name dance. She snapped her gaze up to his face and he shot her a smug smile and a wink as he finished his call to his daughter. "Sounds good. Love you too. Bye." He set his phone down, made a show of stretching his arms over his head, displaying all that blatant male power that made her mouth go dry.

She huffed in irritation. "Stop showing off and finish getting dressed. We're late."

"We're fine. And that," he said, looking pointedly over at the rumpled king-size bed, "was so worth being late for." That hot blue gaze came back to slide over the length of her body.

Yeah, she didn't regret it either. "Is Janelle looking forward to staying with us?" she asked, to get him on track.

Because of the nature of his work as a security contractor and him being out of the country a lot, his ex-wife had initially gotten full custody after their divorce, but things had improved a lot between them over the years and they were civil to each other now. Gage called Janelle at least a couple times a week, and since he'd taken a mostly administrative role with Titanium, he got to see her a lot more often now than he had when she was young.

"Sounds like it."

"Is the boyfriend coming?"

"Nope. She dumped his ass last week because he didn't return some text she sent." He shook his head. "How the hell that generation expects to make a relationship work through texting is a fucking mystery, but I'm not torn up that she ditched the asshole."

"To you, all the guys she dates are assholes," she pointed out in a wry tone, well acquainted with his fondness for using the F-bomb. A habit left over from his days as a master sergeant in Special Forces.

"That's because they are." He faced the mirror as he expertly did up his bowtie.

She took a moment to enjoy the view. The man looked every bit as delicious from the back as he did from the front. Sometimes it was still hard to believe he was hers. "Sooner or later, you're going to have to dial back the whole overprotective dad thing, or she'll start hiding her relationships from you."

He scowled as he straightened the tie. "I've still got time. Besides, she tells you everything anyway. I'll just get it out of you later."

"I'm not your spy, Gage. I wouldn't betray her confidence like that." Well, not unless it was really important.

Gage grunted and didn't bother replying.

At first it had been hard to accept that they couldn't have children of their own because of his vasectomy, but not anymore. Gage had told her he would look into adoption with her if she really wanted to have a child, but she could tell that becoming a parent again wasn't high on his priority list. The man was twelve years older than her, so she understood why he wasn't too keen on going back to the parenting starting line all over again at this point in his life.

Since they'd gotten married she'd made peace with all of that. They had Janelle, who had thankfully accepted Claire as a stepmom with open arms, so it wasn't like she'd completely missed out on being a parent. And the truth was, she liked having time for just the two of them.

Things always happened for a reason. If she was honest, for now at least, Claire was happy with their life just the way it was.

But she'd be a lot more relaxed once they made it to the gala on time.

"Come on," she said, holding out her arm. "Escort your wife downstairs and put her into a cab so she can stop stressing and have a good time tonight."

He raised his red-gold eyebrows at her. "You saying you didn't have a good time already?" He glanced pointedly toward the bed. The duvet and top sheet were lying crumpled in a heap on the floor, and the pillows were scattered haphazardly all over the place.

She made an exasperated sound and slipped her arm through his, her hand nestled between the bend in his elbow and the bulge of his biceps. "You know what I mean."

He grinned and reached for the door. "Yeah, you mean you're a greedy little thing and can't wait for a replay once we get back."

Claire didn't bother gracing that one with a response as they stepped out into the hall.

But he wasn't wrong.

CHAPTER THREE

T he temperature had dropped fast over the past couple hours, and the bitterly cold air was like a blade in his lungs every time he took a breath.

Rob Crossley stood outside the fancy convention center in midtown Manhattan and shoved his gloved hands deeper into his jacket pockets. He'd found out about this gala a couple months ago, and had begun formulating his plan. It had taken him two full days to get to NYC by bus from Atlanta. Only a few more hours to go until he pulled off this operation.

He'd been waiting out here at different intervals all fucking day, watching people come and go. Watching near the back entrance as the caterer and decorator showed up with their crews. Keeping an eye out for his targets and trying to figure out how the security around here worked.

This morning he'd even spotted Khalia Patterson entering the hotel lobby. He'd been so overcome with rage at the sight of her he'd almost reached for the pistol tucked out of sight beneath his jacket, but had thought better of it and reined the impulse in at the last moment. A good thing.

Now he stood in the shadows in the corner of the building close to the front entrance. He was dressed to blend in, wearing a heavy brown jacket and black knit cap, and there were so many people around he didn't draw notice by hanging out around the convention center. Yeah there were a crazy number of CCTVs and other security measures in this city, but he didn't care. He was here for one purpose and one purpose only.

Revenge.

Tonight's event started at seven sharp. The guests had begun to arrive a few minutes ago. A lot of rich people dressed in expensive tuxes and gowns, and fellow veterans in their full dress uniforms. They'd all walked right past him, not even noticing him standing out here in the cold. Having no idea what he'd gone through. All he'd sacrificed, everything he'd suffered for them and this country—and for what?

The entire world treated him like he was invisible. Like a nothing.

Seething inside, he watched the fancy-dressed people pass by him and enter the warmth of the convention center, where a hot, extravagant meal and expensive booze awaited them. They would all sit there eating their fifty-dollar-a-plate meals and listen to the speeches given by the fucking hypocrites who had founded this so-called charity. They would clap and cheer and congratulate themselves on being part of something so wonderful, tell themselves that they were making a difference in veterans' lives.

Fuck. Them.

Those same people putting on tonight's gala were the ones who should have helped him. He'd watched his teammates get blown up and die right in front of him. He still carried shrapnel in his body. He'd come home to recover, and since getting a medical discharge from the Army, he didn't fit in to society anymore. The things he'd seen and done and gone through had changed him too much.

He'd needed help. After a year of struggling with trying to deal with the bureaucratic bullshit that was the VA and battling his growing addiction to his pain meds, he'd woken up one morning wishing he was dead and realized he needed to get help. It had taken all of his courage to admit he wasn't okay and begin seeing a counselor. She was the one who had told him about Scottie's Foundation and encouraged him to apply. So he had.

Only to be shunned by the very people he'd reached out to for help. The organization that had been founded to help veterans like him transition back into the civilian world with funding, counseling and job training. Real, practical solutions that would have made the difference in his life, compared to the pitiful programs the VA had sent him to in the past.

Hunter Phillips and Khalia Patterson were both on the board of directors. They would have seen his application and read his story.

Instead of helping him, they'd rejected him. Treated him no better than any of the other organizations he'd applied to, with only a generic form letter in reply.

He was fucking sick to death of being brushed off and passed over, like he didn't matter. So he was prepared to face the consequences of the actions he took tonight.

Hunching deeper into his jacket, he ducked the lower part of his face behind the turned-up collar as an icy gust of wind cut through him. Left out in the cold again, as usual.

He checked his watch. Ten minutes until seven.

He'd make them sorry soon enough. In just a little while, he'd make them pay for turning their backs on him.

****

Hunter paused in the middle of his conversation with a double amputee Marine vet when a familiar, deep voice cut through the buzz of conversation going on inside the grand ballroom.

"Hunt."

Hunter excused himself from the Marine and spun around to see Gage Wallace, his second-in-command, making his way through the tables toward him, his wife Claire on his arm.

"Hey, man. Glad you could come," Hunter slapped Gage's solid shoulder and shook his hand with the other.

"We wouldn't miss it."

He pulled Claire into a gentle hug. These two were the Titanium team "parents", and Hunter would be lost without them. Their warm, affable personalities suited them perfectly for their roles.

Though Gage now had mostly a behind-the-scenes role with the company, he was still the team daddy same as he had been back in his SF days, always looking out for everyone. Claire worked as an analyst for the NSA but she had naturally assumed the role of being everyone's surrogate mother at Titanium, especially the group gathered here tonight to help them celebrate.

"You look beautiful, as always," he told her.

"Thanks," she said with a smile that made her gray eyes twinkle and pulled back to gaze around the room, her upswept light brown hair gleaming under the lights. "Wow, quite the turnout for your first official gala. I wasn't expecting it to be so huge."

"I can't take credit. It's all Khalia's doing." Because she was freaking amazing. He was the one with the advanced degree in business admin, but she kept blowing him away with her determination and business savvy. Her mathematical mind enabled her to handle problems and logistics with ease.

"You guys are sitting with us during the dinner, right?"

"Yep, right after the speeches."

Gage grinned at him. "Oh, I bet you've been looking forward to that for a long time now, huh?"

"I love giving speeches. It's my favorite." This foundation had shown him a whole new world, one he wasn't nearly as comfortable in as Khalia. She had no problem talking to anyone, rubbing elbows with celebrities and telling them about the work the foundation did.

"Right up there with a prostate exam, huh?"

He barked out a laugh. "Pretty much, yeah.

We're right down in front there with the others." He pointed to a table at the front of the large room near the podium, where the rest of the Titanium gang was already sitting. It meant a lot to him and Khalia that they'd all come to support the cause tonight.

"Awesome. Looking forward to catching up with everyone," Gage said. "Course, I hope you're not expecting us to make a big donation or anything. The salaries at the company I work for are shit." He threw Hunter a pointed look.

Hunter's lips quirked. "Is that right? Maybe I'd better have a word with the owners then." Him and his business partner, Tom Webster, who was scouting out a job in Africa right now.

"You should."

He slapped Gage's shoulder once more. "Go ahead and get a drink on me."

"Don't mind if I do." He set a hand on Claire's lower back and began making their way through the maze of round tables to the front of the room.

Each table sat eight, and they were all full. The guests tonight were mostly veterans and their families, some active duty military personnel, private citizens with a philanthropic bent, politicians, and even a couple of celebrities. He'd helped out where he could, but Khalia and her team had worked their asses off to make this night happen.

Her red gown drew his attention, over at the right side of the room where she was talking to a four-star general and his wife. Khalia worked the room like a pro, totally at ease in her role as co-founder and hostess.

He dragged his gaze from her to a picture of Scottie, displayed on a big screen behind the podium. A bittersweet pang twisted in Hunter's chest as he looked at his fallen best friend.

The candid shot showed Scottie dressed in civvies on the beach at Coronado with the sun setting in the background. His buddy's smile seemed to light up the room, and it still hurt to know Scottie was gone forever. He would have loved the idea behind this foundation, would have been way more comfortable in the limelight than Hunter was.

A flash of red caught his attention. Khalia was waving at him, trying to get him to the stage. He nodded in acknowledgement and started for it so they could get this shebang underway.

"You ready?" she asked him when he reached her, squeezing his hands tight.

He nodded once. He'd rather dismantle a nuke blindfolded than give a speech to a crowd this size, but he was co-chair and duties like this came with the territory. Besides, he was doing this for Scottie.

And he had an important message to deliver to the woman who'd changed his entire life for the better. He'd been in a dark place when he'd met her, and she'd flooded his world with light.

"Let's do this," he said, and helped her up the short set of stairs leading to the stage while the emcee got the crowd quieted and made his introductory remarks.

Taking his place off to one side, he watched Khalia take her cue and walk up to the podium, head held high, her red satin gown gleaming in the lights. She was a thousand times more elegant and poised than he would ever be, completely at ease and in control up there in front of all these people she'd assembled tonight.

With grace and the innate confidence he thought was her sexiest attribute, she gave her opening comments, telling their guests more about Scottie's Foundation and how they could help further the cause of helping veterans transition back into civilian life.

Amidst applause from the audience she walked back to him, and he set a hand on her waist to draw her close, kissing her temple. Then it was his turn.

He drew his notes from his inside jacket pocket and unfolded them. The last speech he'd done was at Scottie's funeral, and he'd agonized over those words for hours as well.

Setting his hands on either side of the podium while the spotlight shone on him, he faced the audience and took a deep breath. Sooner he got this part done, the sooner they could eat and get on with the rest of the itinerary—and after this he only had to come up on stage to present awards and smile for the cameras. No more speaking.

He'd been a SEAL for a long time before he'd left the Navy to become a contractor. He'd planned and participated in high-risk operations all over the world, in the worst conditions imaginable. But he hated being in the spotlight like this.

His heart rate was higher now than it was when he went into combat, and his palms were damp.

In his peripheral vision, Scottie's picture smiled down at him. Hunter hoped his friend could see him now. *This is for you, buddy.*

"Scott Easton wasn't just my teammate, he was my brother. He was also the bravest man I've ever met, in addition to being one of the best human beings I've ever known. When he was killed in action three years ago, I knew I wanted to do something important to honor him. Something that would do justice to the memory of such a brave and selfless warrior." He looked pointedly over at Khalia. "But it wasn't until an equally amazing person came into my life shortly thereafter that I realized what form it would take."

She smiled at him in reply.

Facing the audience again, he continued. "Tonight I'm up here speaking to you not as the co-founder of this foundation, but as a veteran and fellow American. The statistics tell us that we're losing twenty-two veterans every day to suicide. That's unacceptable, and it's something we're working to change. I'm proud of this foundation and what it stands for, and I'm proud as hell of the work it's doing to help our men and women in uniform make what for some is an incredibly difficult transition from military life back into the civilian world. But most of all, I'm proud of the woman standing to my right."

He paused while all eyes shifted to Khalia. The room was absolutely silent as they stared at her. "Scottie's Foundation was Khalia's brainchild, right from the start. None of this," he waved a hand to indicate Scottie's picture and the packed room, "would have been possible without her. She's never worn a uniform in service to her country, but she has the heart of a SEAL, and the work she's done and continues to do should serve as an inspiration and an example to the rest of us.

"She's worked tirelessly to form this foundation and make it into the success it already is. Now, I'm not one for flowery speeches, but I want to take this opportunity to publicly thank and acknowledge her for everything she's done. And tonight, I stand here before you the luckiest man on earth, because less than two hours ago, this incredible, brilliant and driven woman just became my wife."

Amidst the shocked gasps from the Titanium group in front of them and smattering of applause from the rest of the audience, Hunter turned his gaze back to her. Khalia had her hands clasped in front of her mouth, and tears shone in her pretty green eyes.

Yeah, she realized what a huge deal it was for him to say these things in front of a crowd. But he knew how much heartfelt words meant to her, and he wanted her to know he meant every damn one he was saying.

He put his hand over his heart, and damned if his throat didn't tighten up as he looked at her. "Thank you, Khalia, my beautiful wife, from the bottom of my heart. I love you," he finished, and left the podium to gather her into his arms for a kiss.

The room erupted into deafening cheers and applause. Everyone at the Titanium table stood up to give them a standing ovation, even Dunphy, and the other guests joined suit.

"Hunter," Khalia whispered, overcome by emotion as everyone stared at them.

Unable to help the grin on his face, Hunter tucked her into his side and waved at the audience once before guiding her down the steps to take their seats at their table where their friends waited to congratulate them.

She was the best fucking thing that had ever happened to him, and he would forever be grateful to spend the rest of their lives together with her at his side.

CHAPTER FOUR

*S*o far, so good.

Blake kept his head on a swivel to scan the crowded sidewalk as he hurried ahead of the others to the curb and flagged down two approaching cabs. The need to be vigilant was ingrained in him, automatic, even though he didn't anticipate any problems. Crowded places always put him on high alert, and midtown Manhattan took that to a whole new level.

He'd come to the convention center early this morning with Hunter to meet with the facility's security team and check everything over in person. The team had kept a low profile throughout the event, blending in perfectly with the other guests from their positions around the room. He doubted anyone else had even noticed them.

Thankfully everything had gone off without incident, but these days one could never be too careful, especially in a target city like NYC.

When two cabs pulled up to the curb behind Khalia and Hunter's sleek black limo, he gave the drivers the name of the hotel they were all staying at, then opened the back door of the first one and turned back to the rest of the group.

One look at his wife and his heart skipped a few beats. Have mercy, she was insanely hot.

In her heels Jordyn stood as tall as Dunphy, that deep purple gown hugging her fit body to absolute perfection. Her rich brown hair was pulled up into some kind of knot at the back of her head, and that smoky shadow thing she'd done to her eyes made the deep blue of them twice as vivid.

What made the whole package even hotter was knowing she could tear apart and rebuild an engine with those elegant hands, and that she could shoot a rifle with a lethal effectiveness that almost matched his.

The woman was damn fine in every way, and she was all his. He couldn't get to the hotel and be alone with her fast enough. As a full-time employee for Titanium, he traveled a ton. Hunter sent him all over the place on jobs. Blake had been on one in Libya for the past three weeks and had just flown in to meet her here last night, so he planned to spend as much time with her as possible before he started another overseas job after the holidays. With him being away so much and her taking consulting jobs, they didn't get much time together and it was hard on them both.

He watched her come toward him, admiring the confident, easy way she moved. She stayed next to Dunphy as he walked slowly toward the cab, Zahra on his other side with her arm linked through his.

True to form, Dunphy had stubbornly insisted on pulling off tonight without the use of his cane, and even though he had to know the women were flanking him in case he slipped or stumbled, he didn't comment.

A few steps behind them, Alex walked with Gage and Claire. Alex had left his vehicle at their hotel rather than battle more traffic coming here from uptown. Blake waved them toward the second cab then stood by the open back door of the first one and waited for Dunphy. His buddy was moving pretty damn well without the cane, all things considered, but the set of his jaw told the real story.

"Lookin' good there, Marine," Blake called out to him in encouragement. Damn miracle he even had both legs, let alone that he could walk after the damage from the blast.

Dunphy's hard mouth shifted into the semblance of a grin then faded as he doggedly made his way toward the cab.

They hadn't talked as much over the past couple months because Blake had been on one job after another, but on a personal level, he kept in touch more with Dunphy than he did the other Titanium guys. Seeing Dunphy struggle like this was yet another reminder that they were all mortal, and that the same thing could happen to any of them in this line of work.

When Jordyn reached the door he took her hand and gave her a private smile that promised sexy quality time as soon as they got to their room, then helped her into the backseat, followed by Zahra. He knew better than to hover over Dunphy, and climbed into the front seat next to the driver instead.

"Can you believe that speech Hunt gave?" Jordyn said as Dunphy shut the taxi door behind him. "I totally didn't think he had something like that in him. Did you, Blake?"

"Never thought about it before," he said. But yeah, that speech had been epic for such a hard, cynical guy like Hunt. Talk about a grand romantic gesture. Now Blake would have to up his game, because Hunter's words tonight had inspired him.

He tried to make an effort to be romantic by sending Jordyn flowers or little gifts every now and again, but he could do better at telling her what she meant to him and how much he loved her. Sometimes even a woman as strong as Jordyn needed to hear the words. God knew it had taken him long enough to see her, really see her, when she'd been right there in front of him the whole time. Thankfully he'd woken up and pulled his head out of his ass before it had been too late.

"And wow on their elopement, too," Jordyn went on. Even without turning around he could hear the smile in her voice. The woman might be low-maintenance compared to most others, but she still loved romance.

"Yeah, that was a huge surprise," Zahra said, wedged in the middle of the backseat. "Did you know about it?" she asked her husband.

"No," Dunphy replied, and that was it.

A slightly awkward silence filled the cab as the driver pulled away from the curb and out into traffic, a few car lengths behind the limo. Blake stayed quiet, leaving Jordyn to pick up the thread, since she was way more talkative than him.

She was the people person and he was the loner, a quality that had probably helped him to become a

Scout-Sniper. He was comfortable working on his own in the field for long stretches of time as a result, though he didn't do much sniper work these days. He kind of missed it, but he and Jordyn still hit the range together from time to time when he was home, to keep their skills sharp.

Even from up front Blake could feel Dunphy's brooding silence in the back. He wanted to make an attempt to reach out to him. "Hey, there was a Van Halen documentary on TV last Thursday. I only caught the last twenty minutes or so. Did you see it?"

"Seen it a couple times before. It's an old one."

"Oh." Okay, what else could he talk about? "You and Zahr still planning to visit your folks after we all go to Alex's?"

"Yeah, we leave Monday morning."

This was borderline painful. "How long you going for?"

"Until January third." There was a pause. "What about you?"

"We're going to Jord's parents' place for Christmas, then I fly out on the twenty-eighth for a job in Kuwait."

Silence, and Blake hid a wince. He shouldn't have mentioned the job.

He didn't bother trying to resurrect the dead conversation. They all knew Dunphy was struggling right now. Overcoming such a severe injury and the grueling road to recovery that came afterward had taken its toll on the team prankster. Blake hated seeing him this way, because until recently Dunphy had been doing so well.

Blake didn't know for certain, but he was pretty sure it had something to do with not being able to be out in the field anymore. All throughout dinner Dunphy had barely said anything except when spoken to directly. His quietness alone was a red flag that something was wrong, and Dunphy had also made only one sarcastic comment the entire night.

That, more than anything, told the real story. Blake wished he knew how to help his buddy, because his heart went out to the guy.

Hopefully the next few days hanging with the rest of the crew would lift his spirits and give him something to smile about again, at least for a little while. And thank God for Zahra. Blake had huge respect for her.

Not only was she a talented cryptologist for the NSA and spoke multiple languages, she was loyal to a fault. She'd stood by Dunphy through everything life had thrown at them, meeting every setback head on. He hoped Dunphy wasn't taking out his unhappiness on her like he had after he'd been wounded.

Jordyn chattered away to Zahra in the backseat, filling Dunphy's heavy silence. Warmth flooded Blake's chest at the sound of her voice. He'd missed his wife.

They'd both been so busy lately, and apart too much while he was on jobs overseas. She still enjoyed doing contract work for the company. Though she rarely went overseas now, every once in a while Hunt or Tom would assign her to a detail with him. Mostly for low-risk protection assignments throughout Europe and the Middle East.

All Blake knew was he was damn glad to be home for the holidays and excited about spending lots of quality one-on-one time with her over the next couple weeks. They both needed it, and he was looking forward to the break, even if it was only a short one.

A brief reprieve from the harsh realities he encountered in the places he was sent to, in exchange for an idyllic Christmas vacation in snowy upstate New York.

****

Outside the convention center's front entrance, Rob's gaze locked on Khalia Patterson's bright red dress the moment she came into view through the glass doors. His heart rate kicked up a notch when he recognized Hunter Phillips beside her.

As the throng of smartly-dressed guests began to file out before him, he stared at his targets and reviewed his plan. He was so damn cold and impatient to act, he'd been tempted to rush in and carry out the attack during the speeches. That would have been way too risky, however, and now he was glad he'd waited.

He'd been worried that Patterson and Phillips might decide to leave through the back, and he would have lost his opportunity. But here they were, mere yards from him as they spilled out onto the sidewalk with their sycophant guests.

He shifted his stance and kept his hands in his

jacket pockets, eager to get moving. Ten minutes ago he'd popped another couple of speedballs with the last of his ice-cold coffee and the effects were just starting to take hold. Elevated heart rate, his mind clicking faster and faster.

He couldn't allow his brain to get in the way, couldn't afford to let it make him hesitate or second-guess his actions. When he did this he wanted to do it through a haze of adrenaline and stimulants. When he was high he didn't have to think about all the shit that had gotten him here.

It was the only time he felt sane.

Pulse thudding hard in his throat, he tracked his targets' movements toward a limo waiting at the curb. Of course. A cab was beneath these rich, high-and-mighty people who had snubbed him.

When they passed by without noticing him, he took it as a final slight and justification for what he was about to do. The driver was waiting for them with the back door open. They slid into the backseat, facing forward. Rob's last sight of them was them smiling at each other as the driver shut the door.

They wouldn't be smiling for long.

Without pause he spun around and darted for the side alley and hopped on the motorbike he'd parked there hours before. The small vehicle was light and easy to maneuver, allowing him plenty of mobility while his targets would remain stuck in traffic.

He checked his weapon one last time, then stuffed it into his jacket pocket and started the engine. Elation rushed through his veins. After all this time planning, he was finally about to do what he'd come here for.

Payback.

Paused at the alley entrance, he waited until the limo passed by, watched as it stopped at the light at the end of the block before pulling out onto the street to follow it. The familiar warmth of the drugs flooded his system, bringing a euphoric sense of excitement and anticipation.

This was it. He was mere minutes away from accomplishing his end goal. Revenge and justice delivered in the few seconds it took for him to empty his magazine through the limo's back window.

They'd turned him away, cast him aside and left him to suffer alone, probably once they'd dug into his records and seen that two so-called "experts" through the VA had declared him mentally unstable. They'd all driven him to this moment.

Well. Soon he wouldn't be the only one suffering.

CHAPTER FIVE

In their private sanctuary in the back of the limo, Khalia kicked off her heels and snuggled up to her husband with a contented sigh. Her sore feet thanked her. Being in those shoes for even a few hours had made her arches and the balls of her feet ache.

All the work they'd put into preparations for tonight had been worth it. The gala had gone even better than she'd hoped, but she was glad it was over and that she could relax. She worked hard and could schmooze with the best of them at events like tonight for a few hours, then she needed downtime to recharge. Being alone with Hunter now and cuddling into his solid frame felt like heaven.

"I still can't believe you said all that in front of everyone," she murmured, shaking her head a little. The Hunter she'd met in Pakistan would never have done something like that.

He angled his face to look down at her. "What, you didn't like it?"

Her lips curved upward. He knew damn well she had. His words had pierced her yet filled her up at the same time. "I loved it."

50

"And that's exactly why I did it."

He couldn't have surprised her more—a public declaration of love that she'd never forget. They'd been together for over three years now and Hunter was *not* the most romantic man in the world. That only made his words tonight so much more special. "That's the second most romantic thing you've ever done, right after asking me to elope with you this afternoon."

"See, this old dog still has a few tricks up his sleeve."

She squeezed the bulge of his biceps through his tux jacket and smoothed her other hand up the front of his shirt, thrilling at the feel of the hard muscle beneath. "Hmmm, you don't feel that old to me. When did you plan all this, anyway?" They hadn't even had time to eat together the past week, with all the last minute meetings and things that needed to be handled for the gala, and then they'd been traveling here and getting everything set up.

"Couple days before we flew in. I got a marriage license sent to the courthouse. We were lucky to get an appointment there, because they were booked almost solid."

"Well I'm glad it worked out."

He murmured in agreement. "It was a great day."

"Yeah, it was." The best of her life so far. "And I think we earned enough in donations tonight that we should be able to help another eight to ten vets. Maybe more, depending on what they need." She'd added up the amounts personally before leaving.

"Awesome."

Yes. She was so happy they'd built this

foundation together. Sure, in a lot of ways it was her baby because she worked on it and Fair Start—the educational scholarship her father had started—full-time now, but only because he was running Titanium full-time, and he was the impetus behind the whole idea in the first place. It filled her with pride and satisfaction to know they were filling a big gap in the system and making a difference in veterans' lives.

"Think Scottie would have been proud of this?" She'd never met him, only heard stories and seen pictures from Hunter.

"Oh, hell yeah, he'd have loved it all. And he would have loved being up on stage tonight, instead of me."

"I thought you did great."

She glanced down at their joined hands. Seeing the wedding band on Hunter's finger was still a shock. Though they'd been engaged for the past two years, they'd both been so busy and content with the way things were, planning a wedding hadn't been a priority for either of them. So when he'd sprung the idea of eloping at a local courthouse on their way to the convention center, she'd been shocked but delighted.

"Since when did you become a hopeless romantic, anyway?" she asked. She might not have actually planned their wedding or anything, but of course she'd imagined their wedding day a thousand times since they'd gotten engaged. Nothing from today matched what she'd envisioned in her head—there'd been no friends or family in attendance, and she'd pictured getting married on a beach rather than a courthouse—and yet it had been perfect because of its spontaneity and Hunter's emotion behind it.

"Since you inspired me to be a better man."

She tipped her head back to look up at him, her cheek still on his solid shoulder. "Now that's not possible. You were already the best man I know."

He kissed her forehead and squeezed her hand. "No. Just the luckiest, because I have you."

She stayed quiet for a few minutes, enjoying the silence and the opportunity to relax. "We going back to the hotel now?"

"In a bit. I wanted to take you to one more stop first. Be a while before we get there in this traffic though."

They'd barely moved two blocks in the past fifteen minutes, traffic was so insane. The hockey game at Madison Square Garden must have just finished and there were a few big concerts in this part of town tonight as well.

"I don't mind. Gives me more time to cuddle with my sexy new husband." Saying the word felt strange. Strange but wonderful. She couldn't wait to call her mom and brother and tell them the news. Tomorrow, because she wanted the rest of the night to be all about her and Hunter.

While she couldn't wait to see what his next surprise was, it had been a long day and she was drowsy. She sighed and shifted closer, the feel of his strong arm around her and the warmth from the heat vents near the floor lulling her.

There was so much to look forward to over the next couple of weeks.

Tomorrow they could sleep in as long as they wanted before checking out and heading up to Grace and Alex's place just outside of Albany. Hunter had taken time off until after the New Year, which was a big deal for him. After spending a couple days with the Titanium crew, he was whisking her away on a surprise honeymoon.

"What am I supposed to bring on this trip you've got planned for us, by the way?"

"Just a bikini and a toothbrush."

"I didn't pack a bikini."

"Even better. You can just stay naked the whole time."

She laughed softly. "Men are such simple creatures."

"Aren't we?" He hugged her tighter and kissed the top of her head.

The limo made it a few more car lengths before being stopped at yet another red light. Traffic was nuts but she didn't care, too lost in the magic of the day. She covered a yawn and Hunter leaned back to draw her upper body against his chest.

Just as her eyes were drifting closed, the sound of a small engine grew louder as it approached them. She looked at the window just as someone on a motorbike drew up beside them next to Hunter.

The man wore a helmet painted to look like a skull. From the way his head was turned toward them, it appeared like he was staring intently at the tinted windows he couldn't see through. Looking right at them, that eerie skull leering at them.

Fear crawled up her spine. She straightened at the same time Hunter turned his head to look.

The man's hand flashed up, a gun in his grip.

Horror crashed through her.

She tensed and sucked in a breath, opened her mouth to scream a warning, but Hunter was already moving. He grabbed her and started to push her flat on the seat, angling his body over hers.

But it was too late.

Bullets shattered the window, drowning out her terrified screams.

****

Sean Dunphy listened half-heartedly to the conversation going on beside him in the back seat of the cab, his attention focused on the bright lights of Manhattan outside his window. He got a good look, too, since they were crawling along at a rate of what seemed like a few yards per hour. NYC traffic was nuts at the best of times, but in December with all the tourists in town to partake of the holiday cheer everywhere he looked, it was insane.

The limo Hunt and Khalia had taken was a few cars ahead of them. When he glanced back, the cab holding Rycroft, Gage and Claire was a few cars back in the right lane. Beyond it, people who'd left the gala and chosen to walk rather than take a cab were already light-years ahead of them up the sidewalk.

Sean bit back a frustrated sigh. Christ, *he* moved faster than this, even with two fucked-up legs.

He muffled a grunt when Zahra not-so-subtly jabbed an elbow into his ribs, trying to get him to engage in the conversation. He didn't feel like

55

talking with anyone, even his friends. She and Jordyn were doing most of the talking anyway. Up front riding shotgun, Ellis was quiet as usual. One of the things Sean liked most about the sniper, other than Ellis being a fellow former Marine.

"Did you know they were going to elope?" Zahra asked him. She and Jordyn were still talking about the wedding none of them had been invited to.

"Nope. First I heard about it was during Hunt's speech." There. Social niceties handled. He looked back out his window. Yeah, he was being kind of a dick, but he couldn't help it. He just wanted to be alone with Zahra.

He wanted to get back to the hotel and up to the room so he could make love to his wife. That dress and the heels she had on gave him ideas. He hadn't exactly been on his game lately in the bedroom, so he was looking forward to making amends for that.

He felt bad that he'd been such a moody bastard lately, and wanted to make it up to Zahra. She'd been nothing but patient and supportive of him. He'd started to slide a few weeks ago, right around Thanksgiving. The whole rest of the world seemed to be caught up in a holiday frenzy. Even the commercials were full of smiling, happy people decorating for Christmas and doing their shopping.

The whole thing made him feel even more isolated and alone. Everyone else seemed to be going about their lives, the world still turning even though he felt miserable inside. He felt like a useless cripple, downgraded to the sidelines instead of in the action with his Titanium teammates like Ellis and Jordyn.

"They sure know how to put on an event. Everyone loved it," Jordyn said.

Everyone?

Zahra nudged him again. "See? I told you you'd have a good time."

"Yeah," he said, mainly to be polite.

Okay, so the gala hadn't been as awful as he'd been dreading, and it had been good to see the entire crew again, but he'd still rather have skipped it. Seeing some of the severely wounded vets in the room tonight was a reminder that he had it way better than some.

It made him feel like a jackass for feeling sorry for himself when he'd walked in and out of there with two legs under his own power.

The loud buzz of an approaching engine dragged him out of his thoughts. A motorbike drove past his window a second later, in between the two lanes of traffic. But rather than continue to the light at the intersection, it slowed next to Hunt's limo.

Staring at it, a frisson of unease twined through him.

"What's this dude up to?" Ellis muttered from up front.

Sean craned his head around the front seat in time to see the moped driver's hand flash up, a fucking gun in it.

His blood iced up. *Christ.*

Before he could even grab the door handle, gunshots exploded in the night.

Zahra's shocked cry echoed in his ears as he shoved his door open and wrenched himself out of the cab. Ellis was already out and running toward the limo as the shooter gunned his bike and sped away.

Sean ran for the limo. Pain splintered through his legs with every running step but he gritted his teeth and ignored it, his only thought getting to Hunt and Khalia and making sure they were okay.

They had to be okay. *Had* to be. He refused to believe he had just witnessed his friends being shot down in cold blood right in front of his eyes, in an American city.

Running footsteps pounded on the pavement behind him but he didn't pause to look back. It had to be Rycroft and Gage, maybe Zahra, Jordyn or Claire.

Khalia's bloodcurdling wail of anguish and despair spilled out of the limo's shattered window and carried to him on the cold breeze, making the hair on his arms stand up. Fuck, someone was hit.

When he reached the limo Ellis was already there, reaching for the back door handle before the driver could make it around.

"What the hell? What the hell?" the driver was saying, hands on his head in shock.

Sean flew past him just as Ellis hauled the rear door open. The first thing he saw was Khalia huddled on the backseat, cradling Hunt in her arms.

"His chest," she cried, her face twisted with grief, tears streaming down her cheeks.

Hunter was bleeding bad, both hands clasped to the wounds on his chest, the front of his white tux shirt soaked red. His golden brown eyes locked on Sean, glazed but aware as he struggled for breath.

Fucking *hell*. Hunt knew it was bad. Really bad.

"Are you hit?" he demanded of Khalia. He couldn't tell if it was her blood or Hunt's staining the front of her dress.

"N-no. Do something!"

Kicking into medic mode, Sean ripped off his tux jacket and crawled onto the seat, aware of Ellis shouting to the others. "Call a fucking ambulance," he snapped out, prying Hunt and Khalia's hands off Hunt's chest so he could tear open the ruined shirt and see what they were dealing with.

When he saw the wounds, his stomach dropped.

One round had gone through Hunt's upper chest, and another through his side. From the wheezing quality of Hunt's breaths and the way the blood frothed from the wounds, both bullets had penetrated his lungs.

Sean had no equipment. No supplies to do any of the normal things he would have, like start an IV to keep Hunt's blood volume up, a needle to try and re-inflate his collapsed lung, or anything to slow the bleeding with.

Instead he shoved his wadded up tux jacket against the wounds and pressed hard with one hand while he rummaged in his pants pocket with the other. He came up with the package of gum he'd bought earlier, and pulled off the thin plastic wrapping.

Working fast, he tore it in four pieces using his teeth, then lifted the jacket away from Hunt's chest and slapped one on each hole. He had to create an airtight seal to have any hope of inflating the damaged lung. "Hunt, I know it hurts, but I need you to breathe out as much as you can, right now."

Hunter managed a slight nod and exhaled, his body shuddering with the effort. Khalia let out a strangled sob and held him to her, her expression frantic.

The moment Hunt's chest fell, Sean pressed down hard on the plastic. "Hold them down tight," he told Khalia, then climbed closer to roll Hunt slightly to the side. The wounds on his back were smaller, telling him the bullets had entered there and exited through his chest.

And done a fuckload of damage on the way through.

"Breathe out again." Hunt did and Sean quickly put the remaining two pieces of plastic on the entry wounds. He had nothing to hold them there but his own hands. "You guys got the ambulance yet?" he demanded without looking behind him.

Jordyn's voice penetrated his awareness, relaying their location and Hunt's injuries to he assumed 911. So an ambulance should be on its way.

And might get to them sometime in the next hour, given the gridlock they were stuck in.

Hunter coughed up blood, his body bucking as he struggled for air.

Fuck, fuck, fuck. He was drowning in his own blood.

"Sit him up," Sean ordered Khalia, making his voice harsh to counteract the shock she was in. If they didn't sit him up and keep his upper lobes available for air exchange, he'd drown before the ambulance got there.

Her tear-filled green eyes met his and she

scrambled to push Hunter upright while holding the pieces of plastic in place, but she was shaking so bad she couldn't move him. Sean dragged his buddy upward, holding him while Khalia positioned herself like a bolster behind Hunter.

"He can't breathe," she moaned, her hands trembling over the plastic film as blood trickled out from beneath them in rivulets.

I know. Hunt's face was already ashen, his lips turning blue. "He's gonna be okay. Ambulance and fire crew are on the way, the paramedics will be here soon and they'll get him fixed up." He prayed it was true.

Khalia cried quietly and kept her hands in place, the heartbroken sounds of her sobs ripping through Sean. "Hold on, baby. Please, you have to hold on for me," she told Hunt in a ragged voice.

Hunt didn't answer, his entire body corded, face strained with the effort of trying to breathe as he slowly smothered right in front of them.

Sean held that pain-filled amber gaze. Hunt wasn't just his boss, the man was his friend, and Sean was going to do every fucking thing in his power to keep him alive until the paramedics got here.

"Here, this was in the trunk." Ellis scrambled into the back with them and tore open a first aid kit. Scissors, tweezers, antiseptic wipes and some gauze pads spilled out onto the floor. Nothing that would help stabilize Hunt.

Ellis grabbed the gauze pads, ripped open the packaging and pressed them over top of Khalia's hands, waiting until she had a good hold on them to do the same for the ones Sean was pressing on.

"Dark gray motorbike, turned right at the light," Rycroft was saying outside to the others.

Sean tightened his jaw and looked at Ellis. There was nothing any of them could do for Hunt now, except go after the shooter. "I've got Hunt. You guys go get that fucker."

Jaw tight, Ellis nodded once and climbed outside, taking off after Gage and Rycroft as they raced after the shooter. Courtesy of Hunter and Alex taking care of the proper permits, they were all carrying concealed weapons in custom-made holsters tonight.

"Ambulance is on its way," Jordyn said, leaning in through the door. "What do you need?"

A miracle. "Hunt can't wait. Go find a cop and bring back a decent first aid. At least a needle so I can dart his chest." There were cops all over this town. Jordyn had to be able to find one and get Sean something more to work with than what they had.

She turned and raced away.

Zahra climbed inside, her face anxious as she took in the scene. "Can I do anything?"

Khalia was so deep in shock now Sean was surprised she could even keep her hands in place. "Next time Hunt exhales, put your hands where Khalia's are and press down *hard*. You have to hold that plastic in place no matter how slippery it gets."

"Got it." She scrambled past him and wedged herself onto the seat, hovering over Hunt, and met Khalia's stricken gaze. She put her hands over Khalia's, waited until Hunt's chest fell before leaning her body weight onto her palms and pressing down with all her might. "I've got him."

Khalia withdrew her hands and curled her arms around Hunt's waist, burying her face in the side of his neck, her ragged pleas to him to hang on shredding Sean's heart. All the chaos around them, the murmur of voices outside and the sounds of the traffic faded away in the tense vacuum of silence inside the back of the limo.

The wheezing, sucking sounds of Hunt's breaths were awful to hear, and they were growing slower, more labored with every passing second. His eyes were already beginning to droop, his jugular veins protruding on both sides of his neck as his body fought for the oxygen it couldn't absorb.

Looking up at Zahra, Sean held that fearful hazel-green gaze as he pressed the flimsy, cheap-assed pieces of plastic to the entry wounds in Hunt's back and fought the urge to rage at the unfairness of it.

There was literally nothing else he could do for Hunt now.

Except stay with him while they waited for the ambulance Sean was fairly certain wasn't going to get here in time.

CHAPTER SIX

Rob's pulse raced, his breathing erratic as he sped away from the scene. He wrenched the handlebars to the left as he raced between the lanes of cars stuck at the light, barely avoiding the front bumper of a cab when it turned into his path.

A strange sense of numbness mixed with the euphoria and raw fear churning inside him, the icy cold air slapping him in the face. He'd just fired five shots through that window into the backseat where Hunter and Khalia had been sitting.

There was no way he'd missed them both. He didn't know if they were dead or just injured, but he'd sure as hell hit at least one of them with one of those shots, but hopefully both.

A lot of people had seen him do it though. Someone would have called it in already. The cops would be after him right now. Time to enact his escape plan, ditch the helmet and hope for the best.

He risked a glance over his shoulder as he neared the intersection and spotted three big men in tuxes running down the sidewalk toward him, plowing their way through the crowds of people. They were too far away to pose much of a threat even if they happened to be armed, and they were on foot. No way they'd catch him.

Zipping between two cars, he took a right and wove through the stagnant traffic, watching for the first place he spotted to ditch the bike. He found it a block up.

He veered right and darted down the alley. Pulling behind a Dumpster, he shut off the engine and dismounted. He pulled off his helmet, his heart seizing for a moment when an NYPD patrol car pulled up at the opposite end.

His heart slammed like a jackhammer against his ribs, the pistol ice cold against the skin of his belly. He needed to keep it with him until he was in the clear and could ditch it. Every moment he stayed frozen meant more time his pursuers had to find him. Desperate as he was, he wasn't stupid enough to move now and risk drawing the cop's attention.

When the cop stayed inside the car without turning on the flood light or the siren, Rob hid in the shadows while he quickly peeled off his reversible jacket, then turned it inside out and put it back on along with the knit cap from the pocket. Anyone who'd seen him would have reported a guy wearing a black skull helmet and a brown jacket. Now he was in a knit cap and wearing a blue jacket. Might give him the advantage he needed to slip out of the city.

The patrol car hadn't moved. Was the cop here for him, or not? His heartbeat reverberated in his head, the sound of his ragged breathing overly loud in his ears.

He darted a glance to his left, toward the

entrance he'd come through. He still had time. All he had to do was make it to the closest subway entrance and hop a train. From there he could make it out of Manhattan and across to the Jersey side, then bus it back to Atlanta. If he got caught and went to jail, at least he'd know he'd made his point. He could live with that.

They should have helped him rather than turning him away. They'd been his only hope.

Hands in his jacket pockets, he kept his pace leisurely and his body language relaxed as he walked back to the street. A film of cold sweat coated his skin, making him shiver.

The foot traffic on the sidewalk allowed him some measure of concealment. A siren started up behind him.

He looked over his shoulder, his heart jolting when he saw one of the big men from a few minutes ago searching around at the corner.

One of them half-turned. Through the crowd their gazes locked for an instant, and a ribbon of fear curled up Rob's spine.

He'd been spotted. Had to get away before the man caught up to him.

He whirled around and ran up the sidewalk, intent on getting lost in the crowd.

****

The bastard had just given himself away.

It had to be him. Alex held the man's startled stare for a split second, read the fear there, his entire body tensing with a gut-deep recognition.

The shooter.

Before he could move, his quarry spun around and plunged into the crowd, confirming his suspicion.

"There," Alex shouted back to Gage and Ellis, who were both scanning the intersection behind him. He took off after the guy. "Blue jacket, black knit cap, heading east," he finished, pointing in the direction the fucker who'd shot Hunt was heading.

Rage pulsed through him, red-hot and lethal as he ran, his thigh muscles burning with the prolonged sprint. If they caught that motherfucker and got word that Hunt had died, Alex might not let him live long enough for the cops to arrive and take him into custody.

The bastard raced ahead of him, already making the most of the fifty-yard head start. Had to be heading for either a subway entrance or the nearest building he could hide in. Alex wasn't letting him reach either.

He bumped and jostled people on the sidewalk as he sprinted after his prey, ignored the shouts and dirty looks he got while he plowed through the sea of humanity. Alex kept his gaze locked on the back of the man's head, but the shooter was already too far ahead and the crowd swallowed him up.

"Where is he?" Gage shouted as he shouldered his way next to Alex.

Alex craned his neck to see over top of the crowd. The man was nowhere in sight.

Fuck. "I lost him. Thirty yards ahead."

Gage cursed and muscled through a knot of people ahead of them while Ellis ran past using the edge of the street. Alex followed his lead, dodging cabs and other vehicles parked along the curb.

Still no sign of the perp, but a bottleneck had formed where people funneled out of a building and headed for the nearest subway entrance. He'd be stuck in there too. Except there were too many people for Alex to pick him out.

Frustrated, he yanked his phone out of his inside jacket pocket and kept fighting his way up the edge of the sidewalk, searching for the suspect. He updated a local NSA team here in Manhattan and asked them to check surrounding CCTV coverage in hopes of finding the guy. Claire was back at the limo with the others, following their movements via a tracking app on Gage's phone. She'd update the police for them.

He and the Titanium crew didn't have jurisdiction here, but he'd be damned if he'd let this asshole get away and leave it to the cops.

No, this guy had just taken down one of their own, and he would pay the price. Alex wouldn't stop until he hunted his target down.

"Up there, eleven o'clock," Ellis shouted from Alex's left, pointing.

He and Gage zeroed in on the direction mentioned. Alex glimpsed the back of the man's head as he veered left and darted into traffic.

Ellis tore after him, followed by Alex and Gage. The soles of Alex's dress shoes pounded on the pavement as he ran across the middle of the street.

Barely anyone bothered to honk at them because traffic was at a standstill, allowing them to get across easily enough, but the suspect was increasing his lead. Out front, Ellis was the closest to their target, but if that asshole reached a subway entrance there was a good chance he'd lose them.

No way Alex was letting that happen.

The suspect reached the opposite side and headed north. Alex cursed under his breath and summoned a burst of speed when the suspect dodged a clump of people standing outside a coffee shop, then toward the subway entrance.

Right now Alex's only thought was getting that shooter and making him pay for what he'd done.

People's eyes widened as they saw Alex and the others racing down the sidewalk toward them. "Get outta the way," he shouted, waving an arm to try and clear a path. Every second was precious.

The bystanders scrambled back toward the buildings, giving them the room they needed. Alex was breathing hard, his heart pounding when he closed the gap between him and Ellis, Gage right behind him.

The man disappeared from view down the stairs.

"He's entering the subway station," Alex updated the team member waiting on the line, and gave the location. "Send it out to the locals."

"Done."

The rat had just entered a tunnel. There was no way this motherfucker was getting out of this city.

Heart slamming against his ribs, Alex pounded down the steps into the subway station, scanning the throng of people heading through the electronic turnstiles. A spurt of frustration pulsed through him when he spotted the suspect already at the machine.

Two steps ahead of Alex, Ellis snarled and took

a running leap off the last few stairs, landing in a crouch and quickly shoving to his feet to resume the chase but the suspect was already through.

Alex reached the turnstile just as the train pulled up. He swiped his pass, shot through the electronic gate as soon as it swung open.

By the time he was clear, he could no longer see the suspect. He swung his head left then right, looking up and down the platform. No sign of him. He had to be on one of the cars.

The train doors began to slide shut.

Muttering a curse, Alex raced forward. Ellis shouted for someone to hold the door of the car in front of them, then grabbed it and muscled it open. Alex and Gage jumped inside and skidded to a stop just as the doors slid closed and the train began to move.

Grabbing a pole to steady himself, he glanced around, panting. The suspect wasn't there, and Alex didn't know which car he was in. People were staring at them in clear concern but he ignored them. They didn't have time to sweep the entire train together, so they'd have to split up.

"Ellis, you work backward. Gage and I'll work toward the front." There were two cars behind them, and an unknown number ahead of them. The shooter had to be on one of them. He itched to draw his weapon. He refrained, feeling naked without a weapon in his hand at a time like this. Wherever the suspect was, he could still be armed and might open fire on innocent civilians in an attempt to escape.

Once Alex spotted him, however, all bets were off.

"We need to find him before the next stop," he muttered. "Dial me on your phone so we can stay in contact."

"Roger that." Ellis pulled out his phone, dialing as he turned and headed to the rear of the car.

Alex's breathing had just returned to normal as he followed Gage through the train car and opened the door at its front end.

"Hey, you're not allowed to do that," a woman called out behind them, her tone full of annoyance.

Alex didn't so much as glance back at her, all his attention on what lay ahead. He didn't give a fuck how many laws they were breaking right now, and would gladly pay whatever fines they incurred as they moved through the rest of the cars to check them.

The shooter was *not* getting out of the subway system.

Gage opened the car's front door. Ahead of them lay a five-foot gap to the one in front of them. Alex scanned the interior of the next one, phone to his ear to keep in communication with Ellis. He didn't see the suspect.

"Clear," he said to Gage, then nodded. He stood watch while the other man jumped across and opened the next car's door, phone to his ear. Gage headed for the front of the car, Alex right behind him. A woman was standing in the center of the rear of the next car, blocking their view to the front.

"See him?" Alex asked Ellis.

"Negative. Moving toward you guys now."

"Copy." At the door he stopped and nodded at Gage to open it. Four down. They were closing in on the shooter.

They would either get the son of a bitch on the train, or when it stopped at the next station.

CHAPTER SEVEN

Hunter couldn't breathe.

His entire chest was on fire, each breath like sucking flames into his damaged lung. Only he wasn't getting any air. Just more pain, and the horrible sensation of drowning.

He was still alert enough to know what was going on around him. Khalia's arms were around him. Had she been hit too?

She was behind him, holding him tight, crying as she begged him to hold on. All he'd seen was that fucking eerie skull staring at them through the window, then the gun coming up. He'd reacted on instinct.

"The ambulance is coming, baby. Just a little longer," she pleaded, her voice cracking.

He hated that she was scared, hated that she was seeing this. He didn't know whether both lungs had been hit, but he was pretty sure they had both collapsed.

He was going to die if the ambulance didn't get there in the next few minutes. He knew it with a gut-deep certainty. And if he had to die, then being held in his wife's arms while he took his last breath was the best place he could ever have hoped for. He didn't want her to tear herself apart with grief after he was gone.

"Hunt. Look at me."

Dunphy's stern voice snapped him out of his thoughts, made him struggle to lift his heavy eyelids. Those sharp black eyes bored into his, Dunphy's harsh face right above his.

"That's right, you look at me and you keep fighting, you understand? Help's on the way, all you have to do is tough this out for a little while longer. I know it sucks, man, but you have to hang in there just a few more minutes."

He was lying. But Hunter appreciated the effort.

It took too much energy to keep his eyes open. He couldn't even cough now, only gasp, his body already succumbing to the blood loss and lack of oxygen. With every sluggish beat of his heart his lungs filled up with more blood, slowly suffocating him. It was fucking torture.

He couldn't feel his limbs but he somehow made his hand move to grip Khalia's. Her fingers closed around his icy ones and squeezed with a desperate grip. There were so many things he wanted to tell her, so many things he wished he could have experienced with her as husband and wife.

Fear and grief hit him like an avalanche.

They were supposed to go on their honeymoon in a few days. He'd been dreaming of stretching out on the beach with her in the warm sun and taking advantage of their alone time together.

He couldn't believe it was going to end this way, wished he could have spared her the trauma of seeing him die in front of her. She was going to be so devastated, but fuck, he couldn't hold on much longer.

"Hunter, please don't leave me," she begged, her tears soaking his neck. "Please, you can't leave me."

He choked on his own blood. Panic sliced through him. His eyes rolled back in his head, all his muscles jerking. With the last of his strength he fought the darkness closing in on him.

No, goddamn it. Can't leave her. Love her...

Khalia's terrified pleas echoed in his ears as his body gave up the fight and the black vortex of death sucked him down whole.

****

Jordyn's bare feet were scraped to hell and on fire by the time she made it back to the limo, but she didn't give a shit. She'd ditched the heels when she'd gone running for help and didn't even remember where they were.

When she ran up with the cop she'd found a block away, Claire was outside the limo on the phone to the cops, alerting them to the rest of the team's movements as they pursued the shooter. Zahra was in the back with Sean, both tending to Hunter, whose head was lolling on Khalia's shoulder, blood trickling out of the corner of his mouth.

"Ambulance is stuck a block away," she panted to them, shoving the first aid kit through the open door, "but the paramedics are running the stretcher here now and the cops are working on clearing a path for the ambulance. How is he?"

"Unconscious," Dunphy said flatly. "And I can't risk moving him."

"Shit, no…" *Come on, Hunter. Fight, dammit!*

A siren wailed behind them in the distance but she was already afraid it was too late. God, she wanted to do something to help.

She whipped her head around to look back the way she'd come, a measure of relief sliding through her when she saw the paramedics and a couple firefighters charging toward them. She'd already told them exactly what Hunter's wounds were so they could be prepared and avoid wasting time asking useless questions once they got here, but they weren't moving fast enough for her liking, even moving at a near sprint. Hunter needed them *now*.

She stood next to the door, shivering as her breathing returned to normal, feeling helpless and useless. A few feet away Claire shoved her phone at the cop and told him to watch the team's movements on screen, then got on another phone and updated someone, maybe Gage.

Jordyn slipped her arms around her waist and looked northward, but there was no sign of Blake or the other guys in amongst the tangle of traffic and pedestrians. Had they spotted the shooter yet? Were they okay?

Dread mixed with her already high anxiety, twisting into a roiling mass in the pit of her stomach. If the shooter had shot Hunter in cold blood in the middle of a busy street, he would have no qualms about shooting at the others.

She faced southward again, began waving her arms to alert the first responders still rushing toward the limo. "Here! Over here, hurry!" Her heart felt like it would explode as she waited the agonizing minute for them to reach her.

Come on, come on...

The paramedics and firefighters rushed past her, converging on both sides of the limo as they sprang into action. Then Khalia's anguished wail split the night, and Jordyn's heart seized.

"*Noooo!*"

She whipped around to look, fear locking her throat shut as she took in the scene before her. In the back of the limo one paramedic was whipping out a portable defibrillator.

Jordyn put her hands to her mouth. Oh, God, his heart had stopped.

"Jordyn! Get Khalia out of here," Dunphy snapped.

She raced around the back to the other side and reached for Khalia. Zahra was struggling to pull her away from Hunt while the medics and Dunphy worked frantically on him. Zahra gasped and fell backward as Khalia's elbow connected with her cheek.

Firming her jaw, Jordyn reached past Zahra to grab Khalia, wrapped her arms around Khalia's to pin them to her sides, then bodily dragged her out of the backseat.

"Let me go, let me *go*," Khalia screamed, twisting and bucking in Jordyn's hold.

Jordyn ducked her head at the last second,

narrowly avoiding being clipped in the face with the back of Khalia's head. "You have to let him go so they can work on him," Jordyn said, grunting as she strained to haul Khalia outside.

"I won't leave him!"

"No, you won't leave him. You'll just give them space to work." But Jordyn was going to do everything in her power to keep Khalia from seeing what was going on in there.

Khalia gave up fighting and slumped against her with a quiet sob as Jordyn finally pulled her free. The change in momentum sent them tumbling backward.

Jordyn managed to keep hold of her as her butt hit the cold pavement with a bone-jarring thud. Immediately she twisted around onto her knees and cradled Khalia to her, pressing her friend's face against her shoulder. Zahra climbed out and knelt next to them, looking shaken, her face strained.

"Clear," someone said from inside the limo, then came the unmistakable sound of Hunter's body jerking under the force of the shock.

Khalia curled her fingers into the cap sleeves of Jordyn's dress and hung on, sobbing in earnest. Jordyn wrapped her arms around Khalia and held on for all she was worth. "He's gonna make it, Khalia. He will."

He had to. Because Jordyn didn't know what the hell they'd do if he didn't. Losing him would shatter everyone, and she couldn't handle seeing what would happen to Khalia if they did.

Zahra wrapped her arms around them both and sat there, huddled on the ground with them while the bitter wind swept past, carrying the sound of Khalia's grief-stricken sobs with it.

Jordyn didn't know how long they sat like that, trying to shield Khalia from the cold and what was happening inside the limo. The sound of sirens grew louder. Then Sean emerged from the back of the limo, his expression haunted, the front of him covered with blood.

His dark gaze fell on them as they all peered up at him, afraid to ask. Jordyn held her breath along with Khalia, every muscle in her body tense.

"They got his heart started again," he said, sounding exhausted.

Khalia sagged against her and Jordyn rubbed her back.

"They're trying to get in a chest tube now, but he needs emergency surgery and he needs it fast. The trauma team's ready and waiting for him. These guys just have to get him to the hospital." His gaze strayed past them toward the sound of the approaching ambulance.

Hurry, hurry, Jordyn silently begged them.

A flurry of movement exploded around them. Jordyn belatedly realized the cops had already cleared a path around them.

The paramedics had Hunter loaded onto the stretcher. Khalia made a desperate sound and shoved to her feet, running toward him. His eyes were closed, his hand limp as she grasped it.

Without waiting the paramedics rushed him toward the waiting ambulance. They allowed only Khalia to scramble into the back of it.

The rear doors slammed shut and it began

fighting its way through the narrow passage the cops had cleared for it, siren wailing and lights flashing. Dunphy reached down to pull Zahra to her feet, then hauled her into his arms and buried his face in her neck.

"Is he going to make it?" Zahra asked, her voice muffled against his shoulder.

"I don't know," he answered. "But it doesn't look good."

The words sliced through Jordyn's shock.

She struggled to her sore, icy bare feet, feeling frozen inside as she watched it turn the corner and disappear from view, the fading siren leaving them in a vacuum of silence.

There was no sign of Claire. Maybe she'd gone with one of the cops somewhere.

Her chest felt like it was filled with lead as she stared at the busy intersection before her and thought of her husband. "Where are you, Blake?" she whispered, and prayed that wherever they were, he and the others were all right.

CHAPTER EIGHT

Just before he boarded the train, Rob ditched his jacket and knit cap in a trashcan. His heart galloped as he moved to the front of the train and stood there fighting the urge to swing around and search behind him. He had to look cool, not give away that he was nervous or on the run.

He struggled to get his breath back as he stood there, glancing to his right without turning his head. Had he lost the men who'd been chasing him? He hadn't watched to see if they'd jumped on the train in a different car.

He swallowed hard, aware of the sweat coating his forehead and upper lip. His shirt was sticking between his shoulder blades and he felt chilled all over. People were staring, he could feel their eyes on him, and that's the last thing he wanted.

He'd planned to wait a few stops before getting off and switching trains to cross into Jersey, but he couldn't risk waiting that long now. The cops would be out looking for him, would have broadcast his description by now.

He'd be on camera right now too, and there would be transit cops all over the place down here as well. Had someone in the control booth recognized him? Would they be waiting to grab him as soon as the train stopped?

Panic hummed inside him. There was no way he was making it to the Jersey side tonight. There was too much heat.

His only hope was that by losing his jacket, he'd changed his appearance enough to buy him the few minutes it would take to get out of the subway and find a place to hole up for the night. But walking around the middle of Manhattan without a jacket at night in this kind of cold was definitely going to draw notice.

The chaos in his head was deafening. He wanted to squeeze his eyes shut and make all the noise disappear just so he could fucking *think*.

He needed time to come up with a new plan, and the panic eating at him was making him edgy. He'd thought he'd been prepared to face the consequences before he'd pulled the trigger. Now he was afraid. He didn't want to go to jail, and he didn't want to get shot.

There had to be a way out of this. He just needed more time to *think*.

He gripped the steel pole tighter with his right hand and fought the urge to fidget. He'd head for Central Park and find somewhere to lie low until he could figure out what to do.

A crawling sensation at the back of his neck made his skin prickle. Unable to resist, he looked to his right.

Shit, three people toward the middle of the train were openly staring at him. Did they see the bulge of his weapon tucked into his waistband?

They weren't the immediate threat though—that would come from outside this car.

Through the window at the end of the train he stared into the next one. Someone in what looked like a tux was moving toward him. A big guy with reddish-blond hair.

His gut constricted and the blood drained out of his face.

Instinctively he whirled around to face front, putting his back to whoever was behind him. Maybe without the jacket, the guy wouldn't recognize him.

A voice announced the upcoming station, and the train began to slow. His heartbeat accelerated, his palms clammy as he waited. The moment those doors opened, he had to make a break for the exit of the station and get out before anyone caught him.

The train stopped. He moved directly in front of the doors and looked outside.

He didn't see any transit cops closing in on him, and there was an exit to the left so he wouldn't have to run past the men looking for him. There weren't enough people in the car to shield him, and not enough on the platform to allow him to hide. When he exited this train, he would be totally exposed.

Agonizing seconds passed while he waited for the doors to open, his heart slamming against his breastbone. A bead of sweat rolled down the side of his face.

Why weren't they opening? Had they spotted him? Were they going to lock down the train and search it? He didn't dare look toward the next car, too afraid of what he might see, and not wanting to give himself away on the slim chance the men chasing him hadn't spotted him yet.

Finally the doors began to part. It was like a starter's gun going off at the men's hundred meter Olympic final.

He flew through the doors and veered left, sprinting for the stairs that would lead him to street level.

His heart careened in his chest when three transit cops appeared at the bottom of them. They were scanning the platform. One of them saw him, nudged the others.

Shit!

He whipped around, intending to run the other way, but the three guys in tuxes were running toward him.

Cornered.

Panic blasted through him like an IED, sudden and powerful.

No!

He pulled his weapon. People around him cried out and backed away, others cowering there on the platform.

In desperation he lunged forward and grabbed the first target he saw—a young woman.

Before she could do more than gasp he locked an arm around her throat and put the muzzle of the pistol against her temple. His hand shook as he backed toward the wall, his frantic gaze seesawing between the cops and the men in tuxes.

****

Gage jerked to a halt on the platform, gaze

locked on the shooter and his hostage. Anger and adrenaline pumped through his bloodstream, sharpening every one of his senses.

The man's eyes were wide as he held the weapon to the female hostage's head. People cried out and scattered on the platform. Others dropped to the floor and crouched there, frozen, watching the tense scene unfold before them.

To the shooter's right, transit cops blocked the far exit. Gage stood between the shooter and the other exit, along with Alex and Ellis, who were fanned out on either side of him.

Got you now, motherfucker. Savage satisfaction tore through Gage as he stared the shooter down.

Trapped, the man backed away toward the tiled wall, the white of his eyes showing. His voice cracked as he yelled over the noise and confusion. "If any of you take one more step, I'll shoot her in the fucking head, I swear to God!"

Cursing silently, Gage waited, shifting his weight to the balls of his feet. Every muscle tensed, ready to spring, wanting to fly at this asshole and take him down before he hurt anyone else. But Gage and the others couldn't act now without risking the hostage's life.

"Let her go," a young man bravely called out in the taut silence, standing mere yards from the shooter. He was dressed in a suit, his fists clenched at his sides while the woman stared back at him with wide eyes, terror written in every line of her face as she gripped the shooter's forearm with both hands. The young man and woman were together, that much was clear.

"Stay the fuck back," the shooter warned, swinging the barrel of his weapon in a half circle at everyone in warning as he scanned the area.

Gage read the boyfriend's body language, fought back a warning growl. The guy was amped, ready to do something desperate to free the woman.

Don't do it, Gage urged him silently. The situation was way too unstable. One wrong move and the shooter would pull the trigger.

Too late.

"Let her *go*." The young man took a menacing step forward.

A fatal mistake.

The shooter instantly swung his gun toward him and fired.

Screams echoed off the walls. Pandemonium erupted on the platform. People who had been frozen or crouched down until now suddenly jumped up and began fleeing.

Gage clenched his jaw and braced himself as the swirling mass of confusion ebbed around him and his teammates. In their panic to escape, people collided into them, bounced off and kept running.

He pushed his way forward, using the crowd to conceal his movements, wanting to get closer to the shooter, struggled to keep his footing as the human torrent rushed past him.

As it began to clear he saw the young man lying on the platform, one hand pressed to his side as blood spilled onto the concrete. The shooter had the muzzle of the pistol back against the female hostage's head. She was screaming her boyfriend's name, tears spilling down her face.

Finally his sight lines cleared. Alex stood a few yards to his left, Ellis to his right. The transit cops stood blocking the stairs with their service weapons drawn and aimed at the shooter, but they wouldn't fire and risk the hostage's life.

Gage's right hand flexed at his side, itching to draw his weapon and end this now. This asshole had nowhere to go, and desperation made him unpredictable. One innocent bystander was already down. Gage didn't want any others to get shot.

Then he thought of Hunter fighting for his life right now because of this piece of shit and frustration warred with righteous anger. He'd love to tear this son of a bitch apart with his bare hands.

"I told you not to fucking move!" the shooter yelled, face screwed into a mask of fury. He was sweating profusely, his muscles twitching. No one moved, sizing up the new situation.

Then running footsteps echoed from the stairwell behind the transit cops. Dark blue trousers came into view, six NYC cops appearing on the stairs.

Startled, the shooter wheeled the hostage around and raised his weapon to fire at the cops but the woman struggled. Gage was already leaning forward, waiting for an opening to act when Alex or Ellis fired. The shooter cried out and grabbed the back of his leg. Gage raced forward just as the woman twisted in her captor's arms.

Cursing, the shooter grabbed for her again, stumbled. It was the break Gage had been waiting for.

He launched himself at his target, hitting the man square in the back with his shoulder, the full force of his weight behind it.

Something crunched in his shoulder.

An enraged snarl of pain erupted from Gage's throat as he tackled the fucker and slammed him into the ground. They hit the concrete floor with a bone-jarring thud, Gage on top.

The shooter lost his grip on his pistol. It clattered along the floor but the momentum of the diving tackle sent them tumbling toward the subway tracks.

They rolled over one another twice, three times as the shooter bucked and struggled to dislodge him but Gage refused to let go despite the blaze of pain in his right shoulder. He was dimly aware of men rushing toward them, shouting.

As they rolled on the floor in an epic wrestling match Gage grabbed hold of the shooter's hands and twisted the guy beneath him. The back of the shooter's head bounced off the concrete.

From out of nowhere Ellis landed on top of them, pinning them both down, and damn near driving the air from Gage's lungs. But he was amped, the crushing pressure of Ellis's weight barely registering through the need to subdue the man who'd shot Hunter.

The shooter flailed and lashed out with his fists, clipping Gage on the jaw. His head snapped back at the force of it, but the pain merely gave him a burst of added strength. He reared back and slammed his fist into the asshole's face.

Bone crunched, the sharp pain in his hand totally worth it when the guy screamed bloody murder.

Pushing to his knees as he straddled his prisoner,

Gage automatically reared his arm back, ready to deliver another blow to the face. Before he could throw the punch, Ellis grabbed the guy's arms and flipped him over onto his stomach.

Together, he and Ellis wrenched the prisoner's arms down and back. Another scream pierced the air as the guy's wrist snapped, then Alex was there, hauling Gage up and away.

He shrugged off Alex's hold, but Alex grabbed him again. "Gage. *Enough.*"

Panting, adrenaline still coursing through his veins, Gage reluctantly released the prisoner's arm and pushed to his feet. Slowly he became aware of his surroundings again. A group of cops was already surrounding them, weapons drawn, pushing Ellis away as Alex dragged Gage toward the wall.

Breathing hard as the cops took over, Gage went with Alex, refusing to take his gaze off the shooter. The guy's face was all bloody as the cops cuffed him and frisked him.

Alex squeezed Gage's sore shoulder. "You good?"

Covering a wince, he nodded, staring holes through the shooter's face. Who the fuck was he?

Maybe it was a good thing the guy wasn't dead, because Gage wanted answers. He wanted to know why the man had targeted Hunter and Khalia tonight. Because there was no way it had been a random attack.

More cops converged on them. Gage put up his hands and told the cop searching him about the weapon holstered in his waistband. Ellis did the same. Alex had his ID out, calm as he explained who he was and what had happened.

The cops disarmed all three of them, temporarily cuffed them while their IDs were verified. Once everything was cleared up and the situation was contained, the cops took off the cuffs and handed Gage and the others back their weapons. Gage's shoulder throbbed like a toothache and his right hand was sore, but it was nothing compared to what he felt inside.

A hollow feeling expanded in Gage's chest as the cops hauled the shooter to his feet and began to drag him toward the exit. The guy was bleeding, had a busted nose and wrist and would go to jail, but it wasn't enough. Gage wanted to be there as the cops extracted every last bit of information out of the asshole as possible.

And then Gage wanted him to suffer a slow and painful death. Medieval style.

Cops and medics were working on the young man who had been shot. He appeared to be unconscious, and from the frenzied actions of the first responders treating him, it didn't look good. The female hostage was kneeling beside him, sobbing.

It reminded Gage of Hunter and Khalia.

As soon as the cops finished their initial questioning and stepped away, he pulled out his phone to call Claire, anxious for an update on Hunter.

She answered on the first ring. "Gage?"

He closed his eyes at the worry in her voice. The dangers of his job had been one of the reasons she'd walked away from him years ago, and after being injured in that blast he'd promised to take a step back from fieldwork. Seeing him charge after the shooter tonight must have scared her. "Yeah, baby, it's me. I'm okay."

She let out a relieved breath. "Did you find him?"

"We got him. Cops are transporting him right now."

"Good."

More than the anger, the edge of tears in her voice sent an arrow of dread rocketing down his spine. "How's Hunt?"

"Not good. The ambulance came a few minutes ago. Khalia went in it to the hospital."

Motherfucking shit. "Was he still alive?"

"Yes, but…" Her voice caught. "I don't think he's gonna make it, Gage."

CHAPTER NINE

Hospital waiting rooms had to be some of the loneliest places on earth. Khalia now knew that firsthand.

Alone in the small room a nurse had shuffled her into for privacy, she buried her face in her hands and struggled to hang on to what was left of her sanity. She'd been in here for what felt like an eternity already and the wait was slowly driving her crazy.

How long until someone came to update her? And was it good news that no one had come to see her, yet, or bad? Hunter was fighting for his life on the operating table right now and there wasn't a damn thing she could do for him other than sit here and pray that he'd make it through.

She shivered in the chilly room, exhausted. He'd been unconscious when they'd loaded him into of the ambulance and had remained that way ever since. She'd been too paralyzed by fear to cry when his heart had stopped yet again on the way here.

Numb with horror as the paramedics pushed her out of the way, she'd held her breath and stared at him as they'd tried to restart his heart, too afraid to even blink. It wasn't until they paddled him for a second time and got a rhythm again that she'd started to cry and rushed back to her seat to grasp his limp, cold hand.

She'd begged and pleaded with him to fight, to hang on, kept going until her throat was raw. Had he heard her even once? It killed her to remember the way he'd choked and thrashed as he smothered in his own blood in the back of the limo. He'd been in so much pain, so panicked just before he'd lost consciousness.

She looked down at herself. Her beautiful ruby satin gown was stiff with Hunter's blood. The smell of it continued to waft up every so often, making her stomach pitch. She'd washed her hands and arms but there was still blood trapped under her nails and around the edges of her cuticles.

Her wedding band glinted up at her from her lap, the sight of it bringing a wave of fresh tears when there should have been no more to give. She squeezed a soggy tissue tight in her fist, more of them strewn around her feet on the carpeted floor.

This was supposed to have been the happiest day of her life. And it had been, up until the moment those bullets had pierced the window.

She bit down hard on the inside of her cheek, fought the fearful sobs that threatened to rip her chest apart. What the hell was she going to do if he didn't make it?

Hushed footsteps came from out in the hall. A second later the door opened.

She jerked her head up. For one horrible moment her heart careened in her chest, convinced it was the doctor coming to tell her Hunter had died. But it was only Gage and some of the others.

He walked straight over to her without a word and hauled her into his strong arms, lifting her right out of her seat. Her face scrunched against his chest, the embrace crumbling the last of her composure.

Gage squeezed her and pressed his cheek to the top of her head. "He's a tough son of a bitch, Khalia," he told her, his North Carolina drawl low, firm. "He'll pull through this."

The words were meant to be a comfort but instead they broke the icy damn that had formed inside her and all her emotions flooded out.

She buried her face in his shoulder and cried, couldn't seem to stop, the sobs ripping through her, painful and tight. God, she couldn't bear this. Hunter was her whole life and facing the possibility of existing without him was agonizing.

Why? She wanted to scream it. It wasn't fucking fair. None of this was.

Gage didn't say anything, just held her tight, his solid hold on her the only thing keeping her from sliding to the floor in a heap. She shuddered as she remembered those awful moments in the ambulance when they'd had to shock Hunter.

The awful, blank mask on his face as his body corded and jerked, then flopped back down on the stretcher. No flicker of consciousness, his eyes closed, face a ghastly gray color except for the bright red blood coming out of his nose and mouth.

I can't lose him. Please God, I can't lose him.

She was vaguely aware of others moving around them, but didn't care, too lost in her fear and grief, begging God to save her husband.

After a while her tears dried up and she slumped against Gage with an exhausted sigh. Her throat was tight and sore, her eyes swollen and there was a horrible burning sensation in the center of her chest that wouldn't go away.

Gage set her gently back into her seat and someone—Claire—pressed a fresh tissue into her hand. "Thanks," she managed, shoulders hitching, then looked up at Gage. She at least wanted to know that the bastard who had done this would answer for his crimes. "Did you get him?"

He nodded, jaw flexing, bright blue eyes hard. "Yeah."

"Is he dead?" She wanted him to be. She wanted him to have suffered.

"No. The cops took him away, with a broken wrist and nose."

It wasn't nearly enough pain compared to what she and Hunter were both in right now. She glanced at the others, looking at them for the first time since they entered. Sean and Zahra. Blake and Jordyn. Alex wasn't there.

"Who is he?" She needed to know that much, needed to know who had targeted them and maybe figure out why. It couldn't have been random. There had to have been a reason, however twisted it might be, and she didn't want to endure the torture of having to guess.

"Robert Crossley," Ellis said.

She sucked in a breath as shock blasted through her. She'd thought she couldn't feel any colder, but she was wrong.

Gage's gaze sharpened on her. "You know him?"

"I know the name." It hurt to talk. She squeezed the tissue in her hands, her nails digging into her palms. Crossley had stood out, red flags of drug abuse and mental problems making him a clear no for their program. "He applied to the foundation for help a few months ago. We turned him down because his records indicated he was too mentally unstable. We decided he was too high risk and recommended him for further psychiatric care through the VA."

"Son of a bitch," Dunphy muttered, raking a hand through his hair. Zahra shot him a worried look and reached out to put her hand on his shoulder.

Khalia struggled to comprehend it all. This was unbelievable. A disgruntled vet had tried to kill her and Hunter? Had targeted them because they'd rejected his application to their program? That was the reason Hunter was lying on that operating table right now, clinging precariously to life?

She pressed the tissue to her nose and mouth, her stomach twisting hard. God, she was going to throw up.

Someone thrust a plastic trashcan in front of her. She waved it away and shook her head once, swallowing back the bile in her throat. Zahra and Claire sat on either side of her, each setting a hand on her back but she barely noticed, too lost in her thoughts.

Guilt slammed into her, burying her under a crushing weight. This was her fault. She'd been the one with final say over rejecting Crossley's application, and his subsequent pleas for them to reconsider.

As a result, he'd followed them all the way to New York City to get his revenge.

She closed her eyes, sucked in a deep breath. God, she'd never *ever* thought anything like this would happen. If she'd had any idea Crossley was this dangerous, she would have reported him to Hunter and passed the application on to a mental health organization right away.

Should she have known? Her mind relentlessly went through everything she knew about him and his case, every step in her dealings with him. There had to have been signs. How had she and her staff missed them all?

"Have the police talked to you yet?" Gage asked her.

"Not yet. I can't until..." She paused, not wanting to say her worst fears aloud. "Until I know what's happening with Hunter."

Claire rubbed her back gently. "Has there been any word?"

She shook her head. "Not since they took him into the O.R."

"The cops and a couple Feds are waiting for you in the lobby," Gage told her. "They won't be allowed in here until you're ready."

She nodded, completely exhausted. "You don't have to stay," she said to the others, her voice rusty. It was going to be a long night and everyone had been through a lot already. "I'm not sure when he'll be out of surgery. Could be hours yet." She had to believe he was going to make it.

Everyone was quiet for a moment, then Jordyn's derisive snort cut through the silence. "Whatever." She walked over to the closest chair—barefoot, the hem of her purple gown all tattered and dirty—and sat, folding her arms across her chest in a way that told Khalia she wasn't planning on going anywhere anytime soon.

There was a bruise darkening her cheek, and Khalia winced as she remembered lashing out at Jordyn when she had tried to drag her away from Hunter. "Sorry about the elbow to the face earlier."

Jordyn gave her a gentle smile and shrugged. "Don't worry about it."

Gage, Sean and Blake sat down too, all of them watching her.

Khalia couldn't stand it.

"Want me to find you some clothes to change into, and then you can clean up?" Zahra offered softly.

"Yes, please. I'd like to get out of this dress." She wanted to stuff it in a garbage bag, or better yet, into an incinerator and watch it burn.

"Sure, no problem." Zahra got up and left the room.

Everyone else settled in to wait.

Khalia was way past the ability to be social. She leaned her head back against the wall and closed her eyes, forcing her mind to go blank. Much as part of her wanted to suffer through the rest of the wait alone in private, she was glad for the company.

No matter what, her Titanium family would be here for her through whatever happened. It was the only consolation she had.

Leaning into the comfort of Claire's warm embrace, Khalia sat surrounded by an unbreakable circle of love and support and waited for news about her husband's fate.

****

Grace's stomach felt like it was made of concrete as she rushed through the Emergency room doors and glanced around, the shopping bag dangling from one hand. Alex had called her just as she was leaving the airport to tell her what had happened. After picking up her precious cargo there for the surprise, she'd driven straight here as fast as she could, cursing the damn traffic that had delayed her arrival.

Turning left down the first hallway, her heart squeezed when she saw Alex standing there talking on his phone. Tall and strong, his dark hair threaded with more gray than there had been last year. Capable. Dedicated. So handsome he never failed to make her breath catch.

And right now he was hurting inside.

His silver gaze met hers. He said something to whoever he was talking to and then lowered the phone and started toward her, his face drawn.

Grace went straight into his arms, wrapping hers around his waist, and held on tight. "Are you all right?" she murmured, just glad he was safe.

"Yeah." But the strain in his voice and on his face told her otherwise. His job was stressful enough, and a tragedy like this weighed on him heavily.

"How's Hunt?"

"Don't know. We're still waiting for an update."

God, he'd been in surgery for nearly two hours already. That couldn't mean good things. "Do you think he'll make it?" she asked, pulling back slightly to look into his face.

Alex's silver eyes filled with pain. "I…I don't know. It was bad. Really bad."

Oh, God. She hugged him again, giving him the wordless comfort of her embrace, and saying a silent prayer for Hunter. "How's Khalia?"

"Not good."

No. Grace wouldn't be either, in her place. "Where is she?"

"A private waiting room on the third floor. Everyone else is being interviewed by the investigators right now. I wouldn't let them talk to her until we get the word that Hunt made it through surgery. I'm still talking to the Feds about everything. She's alone right now, but I'm sure she'd like some company if you'd like to sit with her while I finish up a few more calls."

The knot in her stomach twisted harder. "Okay." She hated hospitals, with good reason. That sickly, stale smell that seemed to cling to all of them took her right back to the night she'd almost died in the attack in Mombasa, and then a few years later, after the sarin exposure in Karachi.

But none of that mattered now. If Khalia needed her, she'd stay. "I'll stay with her until you guys are free. I brought some clothes. Zahra called and asked me to get some."

"Thank you. Did you pick up the surprise earlier too?"

"He's waiting patiently in the SUV. Not exactly the way I'd planned our first night together."

"No."

She kissed him gently then went to find Khalia.

When she reached the waiting room door, she didn't bother knocking on it. Pushing it open slowly, a painful sensation tightened her chest when she saw Khalia sitting all alone in a beautiful red gown stained with darker splotches from Hunter's blood.

"Hey," Grace said softly, easing the door shut behind her. "Alex told me I'd find you here. You want some company?"

Khalia's attempt at a smile broke her heart. "Sure, thanks."

"I brought you some clothes, if you want to change. The selection at the place I stopped at wasn't great, but they should fit okay." From the bag she pulled a pair of black sweatpants and a large T-shirt that read I heart NY on the front of it. Not that Khalia had any reason whatsoever to love New York City after tonight, but it was all Grace had been able to find that seemed close to her size.

"Thank you," Khalia murmured, and took them into the bathroom at the back of the room. She emerged a few minutes later, the T-shirt swallowing her frame, but at least they were clean and didn't smell of Hunter's blood.

Grace took the seat beside her and slipped an arm around her shoulders, hugging her without another word. Her heart ached for her friend.

Khalia didn't resist. Leaning in, she rested her head on the side of Grace's shoulder. "Did Alex tell you Hunter and I got married today?"

Shock reverberated through her. "What? No."

She nodded, staring across the room. "We eloped this afternoon. He had it all planned out before we left St. Simon's, and sprung it on me on our way to the gala."

Grace's heart twisted. It made all of this a thousand times worse. "That sounds…totally unlike him." She pulled a package of tissues out of her purse and offered them to Khalia.

A soft laugh, and she took the tissues. "I know. But it was so romantic. And you should have heard what he said to me during his speech at the gala. I'll never forget it."

Grace bit her lip, unsure what to say, not wanting to blurt something stupid or patronizing at a time like this.

"This was the happiest day of my life," she whispered, her voice cracking. "And then it turned into my worst nightmare." She dropped her face into her hands, her shoulders quaking.

Pain stabbed through Grace. Feeling utterly helpless and hating it, she rubbed Khalia's back and fought to think of something soothing to say. She couldn't stand to see her friend hurting like this, the fear pulsing from her making Grace feel frantic inside.

But a minute later Khalia got herself back under control and mopped at her eyes and nose with the tissue in her fist. Her breath hitched with the last of the sobs, her slender shoulders quaking with each of them. "I know how much you hate hospitals, so I appreciate you coming in here to sit with me and I'm grateful for the clothes. But you don't have to stay."

There was no way Grace was leaving this room, not while Khalia was by herself. No one should have to wait through something like this alone. "I'm staying. I'll stay as long as you need me to."

Khalia shot her a faint smile, then her expression sobered, her red, swollen eyes holding so much sadness it hurt to look into them. "You know what I keep thinking about?"

Grace shook her head.

"I don't even know if he heard me when I told him I loved him that last time before he went unconscious."

"He heard you." She didn't even hesitate.

Khalia sighed. "I hope so."

"He did." Her voice rang with absolute certainty.

Khalia frowned. "How do you know?"

Grace kept rubbing her back, chose her words carefully before responding. She needed to give Khalia hope, something to hold onto through this endless wait. "After I was wounded in the attack in Mombasa, I heard Alex even when I couldn't see him."

She'd known him as Jack then, of course. But she had recognized his voice instantly and it had cut through everything. All the pain, all the terror as she'd lay bleeding out on that stretcher. She'd known she was dying, had been praying for him to be with her, and then he had been.

"I was either losing consciousness or already

under, but I could still hear him. I clung to his voice and used it as a lifeline, refusing to let go because I knew he was there next to me." Just saying it now brought a rush of tears to her eyes. "So Hunter definitely heard you, and he knows how much you love him. And believe me, he'll fight with everything he has to hold on, because he loves you too much to leave you."

"I kept telling him to fight. To hold on for me."

"And he will." As long as his heart still beat, Hunter would fight tooth and nail to come back to her.

Grace prayed it was true.

Khalia was silent a long moment, the nearly inaudible tick of the clock on the wall marking the seconds. "Thank you for telling me that."

Grace didn't answer, because it wasn't necessary. She just hoped it gave Khalia another measure of strength to get her through this.

They sat in silence together while the minute hand crawled around the face of the clock. Finally, the door swung open.

Khalia jerked upright, her entire body rigid as she and Grace stared at the middle-aged doctor in front of them. He wore surgical scrubs, cap, and a mask dangled from one hand.

"Khalia?"

"Yes," she said, rising in a rush.

Grace laced her fingers together in her lap and waited, heart slamming against her ribs. The man's expression gave nothing away.

"Is Hunter alive?" Khalia demanded.

The surgeon nodded once. "He made it through

surgery—"

Khalia cried out in sheer relief and put both hands over her mouth, her eyes squeezing shut as she absorbed the news.

He waited until she'd calmed down enough to look up at him again. "We've managed to stabilize him. It was pretty touch and go there for a while though, and he's still not out of the woods yet. He's in recovery now with a team there to monitor his vitals."

Khalia nodded, dabbing at her eyes with the tissue. "What about the damage?"

"He lost quite a lot of blood, so much his kidneys were starting to shut down. His left lung was badly damaged. We're giving him another transfusion right now and during the surgery we patched his lung back together. The rest is up to him."

"Can I see him?"

"Not until he's out of recovery. We'll be moving him to Intensive Care next. Once he's up there and we're confident he's still stable, someone will come get you. All right?"

Khalia rushed forward and threw her arms around him. "Thank you. Just…thank you."

The surgeon returned the embrace. "It was my pleasure."

"We got married this afternoon."

"Did you?" he said, surprise and sympathy clear on his face. "Well then that will give him extra incentive to do everything in his power to have a speedy recovery and get out of here, won't it?"

"Yes." Releasing him, Khalia wiped her face

with her hands, the tissue apparently useless at this point.

As soon as he'd left, she turned to Grace, and the smile on her tear-ravaged face lit up the entire room. "He made it, Grace. He's going to be okay."

Grace got up to hug her, squeezing hard. "Yes." But still the worry wouldn't go away.

Please be okay, Hunter.

CHAPTER TEN

A persistent and annoying beeping slowly penetrated his awareness.

Hunter struggled up through the weight pressing him down to pry open his heavy eyelids. As soon as he did, he wished he hadn't.

A white light blinded him, sending pain slicing through his skull like a machete. He squinted against the brightness, was finally able to make out the shape of a bunch of machines a few feet away.

The beeping noise grew clearer, and through the haze of confusion clouding his mind he realized what they were. Medical machines. Monitors.

Hospital? He was weak. Too damn weak to even turn his head, and his chest hurt like a bitch, as if someone had opened him up—

His breath caught as it all came flooding back in a rush.

The gunman on the bike. The bullets shattering the window an instant before they'd slammed into him.

He'd been trying to shield Khalia. Where was she? Had she been hurt? All he remembered after that was the pain, hideous and brutal, and the feeling of drowning. They'd obviously transported him to the hospital and operated on him. He couldn't recall the paramedics arriving, or the trip to the hospital. Not even when they'd prepped him for surgery.

Dunphy had been there, trying to save him, then Zahra. Through it he'd heard Khalia's voice over the top of everything. She'd been crying, begging and pleading with him to fight, to hang on.

And he had. Somehow, he had.

He looked down at himself. They'd put him in a pale blue hospital gown. The edge of a surgical dressing was visible just inside the neckline, but there was no ventilator. He appeared to be breathing on his own at least. But how much damage had been done?

He struggled to lift his hand, saw the IV line plugged into the back of it. With effort he moved his hand to his chest, laid his palm over top of the dressing. He winced at the pain there. Every time he took a breath it hurt. Probably the bullets had shattered his ribs, and his lung had been torn up.

A nurse dressed in scrubs and a surgical cap suddenly appeared next to his bed. She leaned over him, her expression composed, and took his wrist in her hand. Checking his pulse. "Mr. Phillips, do you know where you are?"

"Hospital," he managed to grate out.

Her warm brown eyes crinkled at the corners as she smiled, her calm demeanor easing his mounting anxiety. "That's right. Do you remember what happened?"

"Shot." Fuck, it hurt to talk. But if he was awake

and breathing on his own, that must mean he was going to make it.

She nodded once and set his hand back down on the bed. "You're in the ICU now, just out of surgery. You're going to be fine."

Relief slammed into him, sucking the rest of his strength with it as it faded. "My…wife?"

"Mrs. Phillips is downstairs in the waiting room."

So she must not be seriously injured then. He sagged back against the pillow. "She…hurt?"

"No, not even a scratch. She was lucky." Her eyes flashed up to his, kind and calm. "She told us you shielded her."

He managed a slight nod, just glad he'd been able to protect her. He'd been so afraid he'd failed.

"We're going to monitor you for another hour or so, make sure your vitals hold. If all goes well, we'll let her come up to see you once your surgeon has come in to check on you. He's already talked to her, so she knows you're out of surgery and going to be okay."

Good.

"You're going to be with us for a while yet though, and the biggest concern now is monitoring your kidney function and making sure you keep your lungs clear. Because your lungs were both damaged and you're not going to be moving around too much, you're at a higher risk for developing pneumonia. We've got you on antibiotics already, along with some anti-nausea and pain medications. Because trust me, coughing or throwing up after what you've just been through is no fun at all."

Hunter was only half-listening, thinking about his wife. He needed to see her. To touch her, hear her voice again. And he wanted to see Gage and Alex, find out if they'd tracked down the shooter.

"How's your pain level right now?" the nurse asked, efficiently turning to check the various meds dripping into the line that fed into the back of his hand.

"Okay." A six or seven on a one-to-ten scale. Nothing he couldn't handle.

Her lips twitched. "That right? Based on that frog bones tat I saw on your shoulder and someone saying you were in the military, I'm going to take that with a grain of salt. I had a SEAL patient in here a few years ago, so I know how you fellas roll. And that means I'll be upping your pain med dosage immediately."

He opened his mouth to argue but she merely punched in something on the machine beside the bed and then gave him a reassuring smile. "Get some rest, Mr. Phillips. Your wife will be up here before you know it."

The med cocktail was already weighing down his eyelids again. His eyes slid closed once more, the heavy weight of exhaustion and whatever was in the IV pulling him under. In moments he was far away from everything, even the pain.

The next time he opened his eyes, Khalia was there. He blinked to clear his vision, cursing the grogginess from the drugs.

She was watching him, perched in a chair beside his bed. She leaned over him, a tear running down her cheek and a tremulous smile wobbling on her lips. "Hi," she whispered, and squeezed his hand.

One side of his mouth pulled up. That fiery pain was back in his chest, but he didn't care as long as he got to see her. "Hey." He tried to lift an arm to touch her, wanting to wipe away that tear, but all he could manage was to raise his hand a few inches before it fell back to the bed. God, he was as weak as a newborn colt.

Khalia responded by leaning over him more and pressing her face into his throat. "God, I love you. I love you so much." The soft scent of her shampoo filled his nose.

"Love you too." It sounded like someone had cut his vocal cords, his voice was so rough.

"I've never been that scared in my life. Not ever, and you and I both know that's saying a lot, because I was scared out of my wits plenty of times back in Pakistan."

He made a soothing noise and managed to bring his right hand up enough to cradle the back of her head. Yeah, he knew exactly what she'd been through over there. And so he also knew exactly how strong she was.

"Your heart stopped twice, you know," she went on.

Whoa. "Did it?"

She nodded. "Once in the limo, and once in the ambulance. It's all so surreal right now, I can't even believe everything that happened. But all that matters is you're okay."

The wetness of her tears slid against his skin. "I thought I was all cried out from earlier, but I guess not," she said with a shaky laugh.

He hated that she'd seen all that tonight, that she'd been so scared. "I'm okay. Gonna be fine."

She sat back up and gave him a smile so full of love that it filled his aching chest with healing warmth. Her pale green eyes shone with joy and gratitude. "I know you are." Raising their joined hands, she kissed his knuckles.

"What about the shooter?" His throat was so dry.

Her eyes hardened into shards of jade. "They got him. Gage, Alex and Ellis."

"They did?" Hell, he owed them each a case of beer then.

She made a sound of agreement. "They chased him down into the subway, went from car to car looking for him, then took him down on the platform at the next stop. Either Alex or Ellis shot him in the leg and then Gage apparently broke his nose and wrist. So whatever jail cell he's sitting in right now, he's hurting too."

"Good." She nodded, and he could tell from the way she watched him and her expression that there was more she wasn't telling him. "What?"

She shook her head. "Nothing. It'll keep until later. I know you're tired and the nurse warned me not to wear you out."

He squeezed her hand. "Tell me."

After hesitating a moment, she did. "His name is Rob Crossley."

Hunter frowned. The name seemed vaguely familiar, but he couldn't place it.

"He applied to our program and we rejected him. I rejected him, because his records indicated he was too mentally unstable." She pressed her lips together, sadness etching her expression. "If I'd known just how unstable, this would never have happened because I would have told you and contacted a veteran's mental health organization."

No. No way he would allow her to carry that responsibility. "Not your fault. I read his application too and said no."

"But it was my call in the end."

He squeezed her hand harder, even though it sapped his strength. Already he could feel the weight of exhaustion, or maybe the meds, pulling at him. "Not. Your. Fault."

The forced smile she gave him told him she was anything but convinced. "At least you're going to be okay."

"Yeah." That increasingly familiar weight began to pull at his eyelids again. He frowned, battling it, wanting to stay with her, but it was too strong and he was too weak.

"It's okay, don't fight it. Just go to sleep and I'll be here when you wake up again."

He didn't want to leave her for even one minute, but unfortunately he had no choice in the matter. "Love you," he rasped out as his eyes slid closed.

"I'll love you forever, Hunter," she whispered back.

His last conscious thought was that bullets were nothing. He'd fight hell itself to remain at her side.

CHAPTER ELEVEN

Eleven days later

T he last week and a half had been brutal.
Alex stacked the last file on top of his desk
and turned off his computer, then rubbed a
hand over his face. Damn, he was almost cross-eyed
with exhaustion after staring at screens and
documents for so long.

He'd been working nonstop for the better part of
three days, with hardly any sleep, because he'd
needed to clear his desk of the priority cases he was
working on, and he'd been keeping tabs on what
was going on with Rob Crossley.

At the moment the veteran was in a psychiatric
hospital undergoing assessment and treatment, after
which he'd be returning to jail. The bastard had
methodically planned his attack on Hunter and
Khalia, so Alex didn't think there was any way a
judge would deem him unfit to stand trial for what
he'd done. The only thing he wasn't certain of was
how severe a sentence Crossley would receive.

Between that and going down to NYC to visit
Hunter in the hospital several times, again working
via his hands-free device in the SUV on his way

there and back, Alex was wiped and looking forward to a break. Starting right now.

He got up, put the files in the wall safe and locked them in.

"Alex, they're here," Grace called up, the excitement in her voice going a long way toward pushing aside his fatigue. Once again she'd cleaned the house from top to bottom despite his protests while he worked feverishly to get caught up with his files.

"Okay, be right down." As he cleared everything else on his desk into the appropriate drawer, he tracked her movements downstairs across the hardwood floors. The door to the garage opened, then closed a minute later.

Hiding their special guest—who had already been here for eleven days—for the big reveal later on.

He jogged down the stairs, the comforts of home wrapping around him along with the sense of relief that his work was done. The Christmasy scent of evergreen and spice hung in the air from all the candles Grace had lit around the living room, mixing with the mouthwatering aroma of roasted turkey coming from the kitchen. The second one they'd had already this month, since they'd had to cook the other last week and buy a new one for tonight.

Grace was by the panel window next to the front door when he reached the bottom of the stairs, watching outside. She had on a knee-length dark blue velvet dress, her auburn hair loose around her shoulders. A squeal of delight left her when headlights swung onto their snow-covered drive.

Wrapping his arms around her from behind, he pulled her in close and kissed the top of her head. She tipped her head back to look up at him, the pure elation on her face making him smile.

"All done up there?" she asked.

"All done. I'm not setting foot in my office again until after the New Year."

Something like relief crossed her face, and he was reminded yet again that the demands of his job took a toll on them both. Something he was already taking steps to mitigate. "Love you," she whispered, the faintest sheen of tears in her beautiful aqua eyes.

He understood why. Their lives were about to change forever. She was adorable and deserved all the happiness this particular Christmas was bringing. "Love you too, angel." Every day he thanked the powers that be for bringing her back to him.

Two more vehicles pulled up behind the first one. Alex opened the door and walked out onto the front porch into the frigid air with Grace while everybody unloaded. Sean and Zahra first. Sean had his cane, a good thing given the snow, and waited for the others.

"Oh, it looks just like a postcard," Zahra said, looking around in wonder, a bag of presents in each hand.

"Thanks," Alex said, his arm around Grace's waist. "I've been working my ass off on this place."

Zahra laughed just as Jordyn and Blake climbed out of the last vehicle and immediately headed to the second one.

The doors opened. Gage climbed out from behind the wheel, waved once at them, then moved around to the back door while Claire hurried around to the trunk to haul out a folding wheelchair.

"You guys need a hand?" Alex called out.

"Nah, we're good," Blake called back, taking the wheelchair from Claire and setting it up.

Khalia emerged from the backseat next, waved, then ran around to hover while Gage reached in to help the patient out. Hunter's face was tight with pain as he eased from the SUV and pushed to his feet, Gage's steadying arm around his waist. But he looked a damn sight better than he had when Alex had last seen him, and it had to be a relief to be out of the hospital at last.

Gage and Khalia lowered him into the wheelchair, then Ellis and Gage carried it up the front steps Alex had salted that morning. The others followed right behind them.

Alex held out his hand to Hunter. "Good to see you out and about."

Hunter shook it, gave a half-grin, face pale, faint bruises under his eyes. "Good to be out."

He'd badgered the hospital into discharging him yesterday morning and told Khalia he was well enough to make the trip up here. Alex was glad to have him here to recuperate for a few days. Between Khalia and everyone else here, Hunter wouldn't have to lift a finger during his stay, and they'd all make sure he got plenty of rest.

"How was the drive up?" Alex asked.

"Painful," Hunter said with a half-grin.

Yeah, being buckled into a seatbelt and having to

ride over bumps and through turns while nursing broken ribs and chest incisions didn't sound like a whole lot of fun to Alex. "Go on in and make yourselves comfy, put your feet up for a while." And if he knew Khalia, she'd have a pain pill down Hunter's throat within seconds of getting him settled.

Alex stepped aside to let Ellis wheel Hunter past him and into the living room. Khalia followed, already digging in her purse and coming up with a prescription vial. Gage and Claire each carried in a box of food from their car, Jordyn carrying another and Sean held a bag of gifts in one hand.

Zahra lingered behind the others, her hazel-green eyes alight with excitement, cheeks flushed pink from the cold. "Hi," she gushed, hugging him and Grace. "This place really does look amazing, and it totally suits you. I can't wait to see the view of the lake." Then, in a low murmur, "So, you ready to spring the surprise?"

"Grace is about to burst at the seams," he told her, kissing his almost-daughter on the top of her head.

But he and Grace had a surprise of their own to spring on everyone today. One they'd been waiting to announce for a long time.

Sharing a secret smile with his wife as Zahra entered the house, he caught Grace's hand there on the welcome mat and raised it to his lips for a kiss. "You ready?"

She all but glowed with happiness standing there under the front porch light of their new home, while snow fell gently beyond her and the people they loved like family all gathered together inside. God, he loved her and her giant heart.

"Yes," she said. "I can't wait to see their faces when we tell them."

"Me either."

After everyone was inside with shoes and coats off, they settled on the huge sectional in front of the fireplace while the big tree sparkled in the corner. He and Gage went back out to grab the last of the food Claire had brought up from the city, then left her and Grace to do the last minute prep on the meal while he played bartender.

After pouring Grace and Claire a glass of wine each and handing them over, the two women kicked him out of the kitchen. Knowing better than to waste his breath arguing, he grabbed two mugs of spiced hot apple cider from the crockpot before joining everyone in the living room.

"Here," he said to Hunter, handing him one. He looked more relaxed already, sitting in the plush leather recliner beside the fireplace with his long legs stretched out in front of him. "Merry Christmas."

Hunter's lips twitched. "What, no whipped cream?"

"Wow, talk about high maintenance."

"My mom always served it with whipped cream."

"That's been reserved exclusively for the pumpkin pie, I'm afraid. Grace would stab me with the meat fork if I tried to pilfer any for your hot cider."

"Oh, come on, Grace would give me all the

whipped cream I wanted right now, and you know it. You just don't want to drag your lazy ass back into the kitchen to get me some," Hunter joked.

"Yeah, and too bad for you."

"Nice digs you guys got here," Gage said to him, over on the far right of the sectional next to Zahra and Sean. "That view is something else," he added, nodding toward the bank of windows at the far end of the room. The living room, dining room and master bedroom all overlooked the lake below.

"Yeah, not too shabby," he said, sipping at his drink. Okay, this place had been worth every penny they'd put into it. Grace had done a phenomenal job with everything from the renos she'd wanted, to paint color and furnishings, and the decorations. It looked freaking magical in here.

Without a doubt, the view was Alex's favorite thing about the property. He was looking forward to enjoying cold beers out on the back patio by the pool when the weather warmed up next spring, and cuddling up next to Grace to stare out at the lake together in the evenings while sitting by the outdoor fireplace.

Yeah, scaling things back at work was definitely the right decision. He was fifty-four, and Grace was forty-eight. Even without the major life transition they were about to go through, it was time they both slowed down and enjoyed their life anyhow.

Alex took another recliner on the other side of the fireplace from Hunter and sank back into the soft leather. It was nice having everyone here to spend time together. They all visited for a while, then Grace and Claire emerged from the kitchen.

"Dinner's just about ready to serve," Grace said with a wide smile that made Alex grin.

His wife was in her freaking element right now. She'd always dreamed of having a big family Christmas like this with a crowd of hungry people to feed and spoil. Nothing made her happier than getting the chance to play hostess, and it was even better when it was for people she cared about. Her warmth was imbued in every single room in this house, even his man cave of an office, which had a few little touches that were pure Grace.

"I can't wait," Hunter said. "Been looking forward to this for days now, because I haven't eaten anything decent in almost two weeks. I'm convinced the food they feed people in hospital kills them." He made a face.

"Hey, I snuck you in all kinds of things while you were in there," Khalia protested, seated next to him on a chair from the dining room. "You think it was easy getting that Chipotle bowl past the ICU charge nurse?"

"You're the only reason I'm still alive," he said, grasping her hand and linking their fingers together.

"So," Zahra said with a clap of her hands, announcing a change of subject. "Present time?" She was practically bouncing in her seat.

Alex looked over at Grace, still standing in the entryway, removing her apron. Every single present under the tree had been carefully and lovingly wrapped, then trimmed with ribbon by her own hands.

Except for one. And for all he knew it probably had a bow on it as well, out there in the heated garage.

"Should we? Or should we wait until after dinner?" he asked her.

"After."

Zahra's face fell and Grace laughed. "Look at the bright side, Zahr. It took me three days to prep and cook everything, and once we sit down at the table, it'll all be over in twenty minutes."

CHAPTER TWELVE

S ean sat back on the leather sectional with a groan, stuffed full and more relaxed than he'd been in a damn long time, enjoying the company and the warmth around him. "Man, that was so worth driving here for."

Blake chuckled. "The mountain air sure did do wonders for your appetite."

"I know." He'd had three helpings of pretty much everything on the table. He didn't know what it was about being here, but it was like Grace had infused the air with holiday magic.

Man, his mom would be in her glory here. He'd have to take a bunch of pictures later, so he could show her once he and Zahra got to Coeur D'Alene. And though he'd never admit it, the feast Grace and Claire had prepared was even better than the spread his mom put on.

Everyone else began to filter in from the dining room. He edged closer to the recliner Hunter had vacated earlier and quickly made an adjustment or two before anyone noticed.

He bit down on the inside of his cheek and schooled his expression to hide his grin. God, it had been forever since he'd felt this good. His mischievous streak hadn't shown itself in a long while. High time it made another appearance.

When Zahra came in with a glass of wine in her hand and excitement sparkling in her hazel-green eyes, he tugged her down into his lap. "You look like a kid on Christmas morning," he murmured, dropping a kiss on her upturned mouth. *And I feel like one.*

He didn't know what his wife had been cooking up over the past few weeks, but it had to be something big. She was still really good at hiding her emotions, but he knew her as well as he knew himself by now, and could read her like no one else could. Something was definitely up.

"Well, this is like Christmas morning," she said, nestling into him with her head on his shoulder. "It's more special, having everyone else here with us."

It really was.

He ran his fingers through her hair, savoring the feel of her tucked up against him. Things had been way better between him and Zahra since the night Hunter was shot. Seeing his buddy on the verge of death like that had been one hell of a wakeup call. Zahra had gone through the same hell Khalia had the other night, back when Sean had been hit by the IED that had almost cost him his legs.

Eleven nights ago, Sean had finally realized what that must have been like for her. The helplessness, the fear and grief.

Even during his recovery when he'd pushed her away out of anger, frustration and self-pity, she hadn't budged. On the night of the shooting, it was like he'd seen her through fresh eyes somehow. That didn't excuse the way he'd been in the weeks leading up to it. He wanted to make it up to her.

Zahra had been there for him every moment in the aftermath of the shooting, while he was still covered in Hunt's blood. She'd stood with him and held him in the cold after the ambulance drove away, and had gone to the hospital after to wait with him.

Later, when they'd gotten to their hotel, she'd walked straight into the shower with him and washed him clean with her gentle, loving hands. He'd made love to her twice that night, before falling asleep with her tucked close against him.

For the first time in a long time, that night he'd fallen asleep counting his blessings rather than his hardships. The next morning when he'd woken up, the dark, heavy feeling inside him had been gone. Hunter getting shot had put everything into sharp perspective again. Zahra seemed less stressed too now that things had improved between them. Sean felt like he'd turned the corner again, and he was damn grateful for that.

Gage and Claire walked in from the dining room and settled beside him, then Blake and Jordyn. Khalia walked in with her arm around Hunter's waist, slowly leading him toward the others. Hunt was moving pretty well, all things considered, and he'd eaten a fair amount at dinner. Both good signs that he was on the mend.

And that absolved Sean of feeling any guilt for what was about to happen.

"No, here," he said when Khalia headed for the

sectional, reaching out to shift the recliner Hunter had been in earlier. "It'll be easier for him to get in and out of this, and he can put his feet up."

"Well I gotta be honest and admit your sudden concern for my comfort makes me a little nervous, Dunphy," Hunter said, but allowed Khalia to escort him over. All in all, he looked good for a guy who'd almost died last week, but he'd be damn sore for a while yet.

Sean didn't envy him that part of the recovery, remembering all too well the endless days and nights of pain while his body had healed. They'd been some of the hardest, blackest days of his life.

Grace breezed in, towing Alex by the hand. "*Now* it's present time. Go play Santa," she told him, giving him a little push toward the tree.

"So bossy," he said with a smirk, but did as he was told and hunkered down next to the sparkling Christmas tree. "Which one do you want me to—"

A loud farting noise filled the room.

Alex blinked and everyone turned to stare at Hunter, who sat frozen in his chair, hands still on the armrests.

So freaking awesome. Sean bit down on the inside of his cheek to keep from laughing, the muscles in his belly jerking with the effort of holding it in.

In the ensuing silence, Hunter turned his head to stare at Sean, his dark eyebrows crashing together in a fierce scowl. Glaring, he reached beneath him to pull out the whoopee cushion Sean had placed there.

Unable to hold back a moment longer, Sean

burst out laughing, slapping his thigh with his free hand. It was too good, the timing perfect. He hadn't lost his touch after all. "Gotcha."

Everyone started laughing along with him, and Hunter's lips quivered as he fought a grudging smile. Then a laugh burst out of him and he put a hand to his ribs as he grimaced. "Ow," he muttered, hunching over a little. "That *hurts*, you bastard."

"Dude, laughter's the best medicine."

"Not when you've got busted ribs. Prick." There was no heat in his tone, and in his eyes Sean thought he saw a mixture of respect and maybe even relief.

Another reminder to Sean that everyone here cared about him and had been worried by his withdrawal lately. He sobered at the thought, his smile dying away.

"Okay, well, thank you for that, Sean," Alex said dryly from next to the tree. "Now that the entertainment's been taken care of for the night, let's do this before Grace and Zahra keel over from the anticipation." He knelt and began handing out gifts to everyone.

Sean got an ugly Christmas sweater from Blake and Jordyn, and a new cane hand-painted to resemble Eddie Van Halen's famous red, white and black Frankenstrat guitar from Alex and Grace.

Grinning, he tugged the sweater on and took a turn about the room with his new cane. He hated having to use one, but at least now he could look cool while he did. "This is awesome. Where did you find it?" he asked Alex, who pointed to Grace without looking up from the remaining presents he was digging through under the tree.

She shrugged. "Found an artist online who painted canes, and commissioned it."

"I love it, thank you," he said, pulling her into a hug.

"You're welcome, glad you like it. The sweater suits you, by the way."

"It totally does. Thanks, Blake and Jordyn."

Blake winked at him. "Thought of you the moment we saw it."

Sitting back down beside Zahra, he set his cane aside while she opened up her gifts—a bottle of her favorite perfume from Khalia, and a framed picture of him and Zahra with Alex and Grace while on vacation together in the Bahamas last year.

Her whole face lit up when she saw it. "Oh, I love this! Thank you."

Alex and Grace meant the world to her. She'd had a shitty upbringing and more trauma with her family than anyone should have to bear. Alex had been like a father figure to her these past few years, and having Grace helped fill the empty void of losing her own mother to a horrific death. Sean loved them both to death for opening their hearts to his wife.

While everyone opened gifts and joked around, Sean eased back against the comfy leather and took it all in. The people surrounding him might not be related to him by blood, but they were his family just the same.

"And it looks like there's one more little thing for each couple under here," Alex said.

"Who from?" Hunter asked.

Alex looked at the packages. "Doesn't say." He began passing out little boxes wrapped in shiny silver paper with a red satin bow on top.

Sean handed it to Zahra for her to open. She tugged the bow undone, then meticulously began peeling the tape away from the end flap on the paper. He squelched the urge to snatch it and tear it open. The way she unwrapped gifts drove him nuts, but she'd told him it was because she hadn't gotten many presents as a kid, and she liked to save the pretty paper.

From a nest of red tissue paper, Zahra lifted out a little tree ornament and turned it to face her. Sean leaned over to see better. It read *Baby's First Christmas*, and it had a picture of an infant dressed in pink on it.

Wait, someone was pregnant? If not, he so didn't get it.

He looked at Zahra, who shrugged in bewilderment and looked across at Jordyn.

Then the silence in the room registered. Everyone sat frozen, looking around at everyone else. Jordyn shook her head and glanced around. It couldn't be Claire, because Gage had gotten snipped years ago, and Sean didn't think it was Khalia...

His gaze skipped past Alex to Grace, who was sitting on her knees next to her husband. She was smiling, and there were tears in her eyes. Proud tears.

Everyone gasped and Zahra's hands flew to her mouth in shock as Alex smiled and wrapped his arm around Grace's shoulders. "We're going to be the parents of a three-month-old baby girl we adopted. Her name's Sarah Grace, and we're bringing her home on Monday. We want you all to be her honorary aunts and uncles." He shifted his gaze to Zahra. "And we want you to be her big sister."

Everyone erupted into shouts and claps and congratulations. Zahra looked on the edge of crying as she jumped from her seat and knelt down to catch them both in a huge hug. "I'd be honored to be her big sister. Oh my God, I can't believe this." She pulled back, glared at them. "Wait, how long have you known about this? You never said a thing!"

"We wanted it to be a surprise, and to announce it to all of you at the same time," Grace answered, wiping happy tears from her cheeks.

"Alex, you sly dog," Gage called out. "This mean you're retiring?"

"I'm scaling back right now, but yeah. In another year or two." He looked into Grace's face. "I want to devote all my time to my girls."

Holy shit. That was just as much a bombshell as the baby announcement.

Sean pushed to his feet, forgoing his awesome new cane, and shook Alex's hand. "Congrats, man. I'm happy for you guys."

Those silver eyes warmed with genuine affection. "Thanks."

Next he dragged Grace into his arms. He thought of the emergency hysterectomy the terrorist attack had forced upon her, and damned if something didn't ache in his chest at the thought of her finally getting the chance to be a mother. "This is incredible news. Sarah's one lucky little girl, to have you for a mama."

She returned the hug then pushed back a moment later, blinking fast. "Don't make me cry again. Now," she said, looking at Zahra. "I think we've got one more surprise in store for tonight, don't we?"

"Yes, I think you're right. Be right back." Zahra practically skipped from the room, the slight hitch in her stride making Sean's heart squeeze. He and his little survivor had been through so much together. He'd never known he was capable of this kind of love until she came along. He wasn't ready to have a family yet, and neither was she, but they both wanted kids one day and now he could actually envision himself as a father.

Everyone was watching him. He stayed where he was and waited, anticipation building as he wondered what the surprise was that had Zahra so excited.

A minute later she reappeared, holding the end of a leash in her hand. He blinked and then a black dog appeared around the corner, with cute floppy ears and a wagging tail, and a big red bow tied around his neck.

"Meet your new best friend," Zahra said to him proudly. "His name's Eddie, and he's from all of us. Merry Christmas."

What?

Stunned, he took the end of the leash from her and went onto one knee as the dog approached, ignoring the twinge of pain in his legs. Eddie walked right up to him and stopped, rear end wiggling like crazy, feathery black tail slapping at the lower branches of the Christmas tree, and immediately began licking Sean's face.

"He's a rescue from this neat program down in Virginia that Khalia told me about," Zahra explained. "That business trip I took last month wasn't really a business trip. The guy who runs the program—Wyatt Colebrook—is an amputee combat vet. He takes rescue dogs from shelters and trains them to be therapy dogs and companions for other vets. This little guy was already named Eddie, after someone Colebrook lost. The moment I heard that, I knew it was fate, since he's got the same name as your favorite musician."

Ruffling the dog's soft black fur, Sean couldn't wipe the grin off his face. The last dog he'd owned had died when Sean was in his teens, and he still missed him. He looked up at his wife. "What brought this on?"

She hesitated a moment, then shrugged. "I could feel you slipping away from me these past couple months, and when I found out about the program from Khalia, I did some research and thought having a therapy dog might be good for you. For us. Besides," she said with a teasing smile, "I figured this was a good first step before we think about having kids. I'm told Eddie's a really good listener, if you ever feel like talking to him instead of me."

He looked around the room, still petting Eddie. "So all of you knew about this?" He was a little embarrassed about being called out on his ongoing PTSD issues right here in front of everyone, but they were family to him and they all knew what he'd been going through.

Everyone nodded, smiling at him.

"Yes, everyone pitched in to buy him and transport him to New York, so we could surprise you at our Christmas dinner. He's been sleeping with one of your Van Halen T-shirts for the past few weeks, so he's already used to your scent."

I'll be damned. He'd noticed one of them had been missing.

"Grace picked him up for me at the airport the night of the gala," Zahra explained. "And after what happened…" She paused, shot Hunter a sympathetic smile. "She and Alex volunteered to keep him here until we could all get together to celebrate and surprise you as a group. He was such a good boy, too, staying quiet out in the garage the whole time we've been here today so he didn't spoil the surprise. Weren't you Eddie?"

Eddie wagged his tail harder.

"And I already told Zahra that you can take him into the office with you," Hunter added. "He can be the team mascot."

Eddie gazed up at him with adoring, soft brown eyes, back end still wagging. Sean was blown away by everything, that everyone had been involved somehow, and touched that they'd wanted to do this for him. He swallowed, his throat suddenly tight.

"Thank you," he said simply, then stood to hug his wife, suddenly feeling more optimistic about the future. "I love you," he whispered, pausing to smooth the hair back from her face.

"Love you too. And before you ask, no, Eddie cannot sleep on our bed."

Sean looked from her to the dog, and hid a smile. He gave it three to five days, max, before Eddie had her wrapped around one of his front paws and wound up sleeping on the foot of their bed.

Still petting the dog, he lowered himself back into his seat.

A loud farting noise filled the room.

Startled, Eddie's ears perked up and he cocked his head, making everyone laugh.

Sean looked over at Hunter, who was grinning smugly at him. The former SEAL raised his mug of cider in salute, and winked. "Gotcha."

CHAPTER THIRTEEN

At the sight of the king-size four-poster bed with its turned-down covers waiting for him when he emerged from the bathroom, Hunter almost moaned aloud.

"Oh God, I thought this day would never end," he said with a heartfelt groan as he gingerly climbed up into the big bed and stretched out under the covers next to his wife.

His very naked wife. The first time he'd seen her that way since he'd been shot. He'd missed the view terribly.

"You did great," Khalia said to him, tugging the covers over herself. She'd slept fully dressed in the uncomfortable pullout chair in his hospital room every night, refusing to sleep at their hotel no matter how much he argued about it with her. She'd vowed not to leave his side until he was discharged, and she hadn't. "Not that I'd expect any less from my heroic and incredibly sexy SEAL hubby."

He grunted, savoring the sensation of sinking into the mattress. He was just glad she still found him sexy after everything she'd witnessed over these past eleven days.

Maintaining one's dignity in a hospital was pretty much impossible. Seeing him peeing into a bag through a catheter for the first three days, then helping him on and off the toilet after that had to be definite turnoffs, but Khalia had never once shied away from any of it or seemed uncomfortable. She had to be as tired as him but she'd never complained and tonight they both needed a good night's sleep.

Last night, the first night since he'd been discharged, they'd both finally enjoyed the comforts of a real bed again. For Hunter it had been heaven, except that Khalia had insisted on wearing a nightie and placing a pile of pillows between them, for fear of her bumping into him in her sleep and hurting him. He would have argued, but he'd been too exhausted and just relieved to be in the same bed as her again. The pain had woken him up throughout the night and she hadn't slept well because of his restlessness.

Tonight, there was nothing between them and his pain meds were keeping him comfortable. Khalia shifted over until her bare thigh brushed his. Her sweet, clean scent rose, teasing his senses.

Blood surged to his groin, the feel of his swelling erection filling him with gratitude. It was all the proof he needed that he really was through the worst of it and on the mend. Finally. He reached out an arm and drew her closer, pulling those soft curves and warm, silky skin against him, bit back a moan.

"Aren't you glad we came though?" she asked, rolling on her side to face him, hands tucked beneath her cheek and draped a thigh over his, oblivious to how turned on he was getting just from the feel of her.

He traced the edge of her face with his fingertips. She was so damn beautiful and loving. She'd given him so much strength and comfort over the past week and a half, making everything way easier on him. "Yeah, it was great."

Alex and Grace were the best hosts, too. They'd made everyone feel comfortable and welcome here in their new home. And even though laughing made his ribs hurt like a bitch, he'd been glad to see Dunphy pull that practical joke on him. Sean was definitely in a better place than he had been the night Hunter was shot.

"I'm still full from dinner," he said with a sigh.

"You sure it's not because of the three pieces of pumpkin pie you ate afterward?" she teased. "With whipped cream?"

He groaned again and rubbed a hand over his full stomach. "Don't mention that right now."

She smiled and glanced around the room with a happy sigh. "Grace really went all out with the holiday decorations, huh?"

"Yeah." They were tucked up in one of the upstairs guestrooms. The quiet was blissful after the constant noise and motion at the hospital. A small tree twinkled softly on the table in the corner, casting a soft glow across the room, and the bed was made up with cozy snowflake-pattern flannel sheets and a patchwork quilt with snowmen on it over top of the puffy duvet.

It was such a relief to be lying down again. His

pain level wore on him throughout the day, but it was the fatigue that drove him crazy. Doing the littlest thing seemed to sap his energy.

Except right now, lying next to his gorgeous, naked wife, he wasn't so tired anymore. And neither was the swelling flesh between his legs. The pleasurable throb spread, turning into an ache he couldn't ignore.

Khalia still hadn't noticed his condition. She came up on one elbow to lean over him, curving her free arm around his waist as she bent to kiss his forehead, the bridge of his nose. The lights from the tree in the corner glinted off her hair and made her eyes sparkle like pale gemstones. "You lasted a lot longer than I thought you would."

He angled his head to stare into her eyes, raised his eyebrows in feigned insult. "You questioning my stamina?" Unable to stand the ache, he caught her hand and slid it beneath the covers to set it on his cock, already hard and swollen for her.

"Wow, someone's feeling better," she murmured, leaning in to brush her lips over his.

Hunter sank his hand into her hair, fingers contracting to hold her close as he crushed his mouth to hers, tasting that smile.

She hummed her approval and opened for the insistent stroke of his tongue. His heartbeat quickened, his entire body rigid with unfulfilled desire.

He needed his *wife*. To be inside her, lose himself in the comfort of her body.

When he would have rolled her underneath him, she protested and pushed against his shoulder.

"Nuh-uh. If you want me to do this, then you have to lie still."

"I don't care if it hurts. Need you," he muttered, leaning in to close his teeth on the sensitive juncture of her neck and shoulder. He wanted to nip and lick and kiss every inch of her, eat her right up.

Khalia pushed firmly on his shoulder, trying to get him to turn onto his back, and he relented with a frustrated sigh. Before he could reach for her again she gripped him in her hand and swung a thigh over his hips to straddle him.

The feel of those soft fingers wrapped around his cock wrenched a strangled sound from the back of his throat. Maybe it was because he'd come so close to dying last week, he didn't know, but the sensation was so intense right now his entire body was going up in flames and she was the only one who could ease him.

Her pretty round breasts bobbed above him, too great a temptation to ignore. He set a hand on her lower back and started to come up on one elbow, but she admonished him and pushed him flat beneath her. The dark curtain of her curls fell around him as she leaned down to capture his mouth in a slow, sensual kiss that had him panting, her skillful fingers milking him with each stroke of her fist.

Hunter moaned into her mouth and lifted his hips, pumping into her hand. Pleasure coiled, dark and delicious, slowly spreading up from the base of his spine. Then she sat up and swayed forward, dangling those beautiful breasts just above his lips.

He drew one taut nipple into his mouth and

sucked, stroking the tip with his tongue. She gasped and let her head fall back, palming the back of his head to hold him close.

He was drowning again, but this time in the best way possible. His mind was a haze of pleasure as he switched to the other breast, reveling in every tiny moan he pulled out of her, his hips rocking his swollen cock into her fist.

She eased away suddenly, ignoring his initial protest as she kissed her way down his chest, carefully touching her lips to his barely-healed scars, and down the middle of his quivering abdomen. With her hand still wrapped securely, she glanced up the length of his body at him, and the sultry light in her eyes made him shudder.

He held his breath, wrapped his fist in her hair and waited the agonizing heartbeat she paused before opening her lips around the ultra-sensitive crown of his cock.

"Oh, Christ, Khalia," he moaned like a man in delirium. "Don't stop. More. I need more, baby."

Giving a satisfied hum that vibrated down the length of his shaft and made him suck in a breath between his teeth, she swirled her tongue around the flared head then sank down on him.

Scalding heat and suction surrounded him.

He groaned and squeezed the fistful of hair he held, his hips thrusting helplessly under the lash of pleasure. Fiery jolts of pain splintered out from his healing ribs every time he moved but it was so worth it and the pleasure she gave him drowned out most of it.

It felt fucking incredible. He wasn't going to last,

somehow managed to babble the words to her as he gasped and shook beneath her mouth. In answer she sped her movements up and sucked harder, that sexy little moan at the back of her throat destroying him.

With the last shred of control he had, he pulled free of her mouth and reached for her, bringing her up to straddle his hips. "Want you with me," he rasped out, fingers clenched in her hair as he dragged her down for a deep, sensual kiss. It had been a while for her too, and he knew she was aroused. He didn't want this to be one-sided, wanted her to enjoy it too.

She hesitated only a moment before wriggling into position, settling the soft, secret flesh between her legs against his rigid erection. Using his shoulders to balance herself, she slid back and forth, rubbing him right where she needed it.

Oh yeah. He loved watching her pleasure herself with his body.

He helped her along by cupping those gorgeous breasts and playing with her nipples. Within minutes she was gasping, her breathing erratic, cheeks flushed. So close.

"Now," he bit out.

Khalia took him in hand, stood him up, then looked into his eyes as she sank down on him. Every muscle in his body locked tight at the feel of her warmth squeezing around him.

She stared down at him through lust-glazed, heavy-lidded eyes and began to rock up and down, slipping a hand down to stroke her clit. He growled deep in his chest and took it, letting her set the pace and angle. Ecstasy licked up from where they were joined with every slick, gliding stroke, flowing up his spine like molten honey.

With a soft whimper she arched her back and closed her eyes, her inner muscles clenching tight as she reached the edge. She was so gorgeous and sexy like that, taking what she needed, giving into the pleasure while he watched. *"Hunter…"*

Oh, fuck. The way she said his name like that, all helpless and breathless, pushed him over the brink. There was no controlling it. He couldn't stay still, couldn't be quiet as ecstasy slammed into him.

He closed his eyes and drove into her, fisting her hair tight with one hand as his orgasm swept through him. He shuddered beneath her as she continued to rock and glide and draw it out, his loud groans of release filling the room.

Totally annihilated, he melted back against the covers. Each heaving breath sent pain splintering through his chest and side as his healing ribs protested what they'd just done.

Don't care. Totally worth it.

Khalia shifted and he realized he was still gripping her hair like a dying man. He relaxed his fingers, stroked them through the thick tangle of her curls instead as she bent to kiss him. Slow, soft, tender. He brought up his other arm and smoothed his palm over the length of her bare back.

Raising her head, those gorgeous pale green eyes searched his. "You okay?"

"Oh yeah," he said in a deep, satisfied rumble. The pain in his ribs was already fading. "You?"

The slow smile she gave him perfectly matched

her hum of pleasure. "So relaxed. I needed that."

"God, me too." He'd sleep like a rock now, could already feel the post-orgasmic lethargy pulling at him.

She shifted off him, then lay down next to him with her head nestled in the hollow of his shoulder, her hand resting lightly over his heart. She did that a lot now, touching the center of his chest, as if feeling his heartbeat soothed her.

The pain in his chest was fading now that his breathing was back to normal. With his arm curved around her back, he closed his eyes and sighed in contentment.

Yeah, he was *really* glad they'd come up here rather than fly back to St. Simons. His mom was already at their place waiting for them to get back, and Khalia's mom and brother were flying in on Christmas Eve to spend the holidays. By then he should be feeling a lot better, but he was glad they'd decided to take this time here to be with the Titanium crew.

The honeymoon he'd planned for them in the Maldives had been postponed indefinitely for the time being. They'd figure all that out over the next couple of months, after he'd implemented a series of new security measures and procedures for their foundation.

Scottie's Foundation did great and important work, but he never wanted it to jeopardize his or Khalia's safety again. There was also Crossley's legal process to consider. Hunter had kept apprised of the legal updates through Alex. It was likely that he, Khalia and the other Titanium members who had witnessed the shooting would have to testify against Crossley at the trial, whenever that happened.

Something he didn't want to think about right now.

"So Alex and Grace are going to be parents," Khalia murmured, pulling him from his thoughts. He opened his eyes to find her staring past him out the window while the snowflakes swirled in the light from the lampposts outside. "Isn't that amazing?"

"Yeah." More amazing to him that Alex was actually taking steps to retire so he could be a fulltime dad and husband.

"I can't wait to meet little Sarah." Her voice was wistful.

He was quiet a moment, stroking his fingers through her long curls. They clung to his fingers, as if they didn't want to let him go. "Maybe we should think about becoming parents soon too." She'd be an absolutely incredible mother. Loving, loyal, protective. He didn't think he'd be a bad dad either, and he liked kids.

She looked up at him, surprise clear in her eyes. "Really?"

He nodded. He knew she wanted to have a baby so bad she could taste it, and being part owner of Titanium, he could shift his schedule around to suit him. "Yeah."

"How soon?"

"Maybe we could start trying within the next year or so."

Her lips curved in a tender smile. "I'd love that."

After pressing a soft kiss to his lips, she snuggled into his embrace. "This holiday season was by far the worst I've ever had, but it's also been the best in a lot of ways too." She tilted her head back to meet his eyes. "Does that make sense?"

"Yeah, it does." He pulled her head back down to his shoulder and held her close, letting the peacefulness of the moment surround him in their private, cozy sanctuary. "I love you."

He felt her sleepy smile against his shoulder. "I know. Love you too."

Hunter lay awake as her breathing turned slow and deep, thinking of how lucky he was. This Christmas he had more to be grateful for than ever.

A strong and devoted wife he loved with everything in him. And a bright, shiny New Year for them both waiting on the horizon, filled with countless possibilities as they began the rest of their lives together.

EPILOGUE

Seven months later

"So he's really going to do it?" Khalia asked Grace as they rocked on the porch swing under the shade of the back verandah, the warm July evening breeze washing over them. She and Hunter had arrived at lunchtime and were going to spend the first three days of their summer getaway with Alex, Grace and their adorable daughter who Khalia couldn't get enough of.

"What, retire?"

"Yes." Down the lush, sloping lawn, the velvety blue lake shimmered in the glow of the sunset. Alex stood at the edge of the grassy bank talking to Hunter, the two men's broad-shouldered builds silhouetted against a sky set alight in a spectacular blaze of vivid pinks and oranges. It seemed so hard to believe that a man as legendary as Alex Rycroft would actually retire completely from the NSA at age fifty-five.

"That's the plan," Grace said, her voice wry as she gazed out at her husband. "Whether it actually happens or not is another story. Even if he does, I'm pretty sure he'd still take on contract or consulting work. Being fully retired would drive him insane, I think."

"Well, he's got another good reason to leave all that behind now," she murmured, looking down into the face of the sleeping angel she held in her arms, all warm and snuggly.

Her heart turned over as she studied every detail of that tiny little face. Little Sarah Grace had a mop of thick black hair and perfect, satin-smooth skin that was kissed with the pale gold of her half-Asian heritage. Her black lashes were so long they cast shadows on the tops of her cheeks and her little pink lips were parted in her sleep. So kissable it was ridiculous. It was all Khalia could do not to smooch them over and over.

"Is she getting heavy?" Grace asked.

"Are you kidding? I'm loving this." Khalia gathered the little girl tighter to her, melting when Sarah shifted and sighed in her sleep. So trusting. So innocent.

"I can see that," she said dryly.

Sarah Grace was almost ten months old now, and from all the furniture surfing Khalia had seen her do this afternoon, not far from walking. "Once she gets mobile, she's gonna run the two of you ragged."

Grace cracked a grin. "We're already ragged. Not that I have anything to compare it with, but I swear she's got to be the worst teether ever born. Neither of us have slept more than two hours at a time for the past two months. It's killing us." She chuckled to herself. "I think Alex secretly loves it whenever he has to travel for work. He's only had a few trips since Sarah Grace came home, but he flies down to Maryland every other week so he can be in the office. Probably can't wait to climb into that hotel bed all by himself, knowing he'll get a solid six hours of sleep."

Smiling, Khalia glanced at her. "Totally worth it though, right?"

An expression of complete maternal bliss transformed Grace's face as she looked down at her sleeping daughter. "Totally. Every single second of it, even when I'm so exhausted I can barely function." She shook her head in wonder. "I never knew I could love another person this much. I mean, I love Alex like crazy, of course, but it's totally different when you have a child. Instinctive. Protective, nurturing and all-consuming at the same time. I can't explain it."

Khalia nodded thoughtfully. "I've heard other parents say the same thing." *I can't wait to experience it firsthand.*

She let her gaze wander back to Hunter, still talking with Alex. He'd healed up so well from his surgeries and was practically running Titanium now that Tom Webster had scaled his involvement back. For her part, she'd been busy expanding Scottie's Foundation and implementing the security measures Hunter had set into place. As of now there were more than two hundred veterans in their program.

"I think we're going to start trying soon." Tingles of excitement fluttered in her belly at the thought. Their baby would have dark hair. Curly like hers? Amber eyes like Hunter, or pale green like her?

A smug smile curved Grace's mouth. "I knew it. I could see the signs of baby fever all over you the moment you stepped onto our front porch."

She laughed softly. "Can't deny it." She stroked her fingers over Sarah Grace's fuzzy hair, fighting the urge to squish her. "God, I could just eat her up."

Grace tutted. "Yep, that's a classic, end-stage symptom. I'm afraid there's no saving you now." Laughter shaded her voice.

Khalia couldn't wipe the contented smile off her face as she looked back at her husband. "Nope. I'm a goner, for sure."

All she knew was, she was one lucky woman, and couldn't wait to start trying for a family of their own.

—The End—

Thank you for reading BLINDSIDED: A TITANIUM CHRISTMAS NOVELLA. I really hope you enjoyed it and that you'll consider leaving a review at one of your favorite online retailers. It's a great way to help other readers discover new books.

If you liked BLINDSIDED and would like to read more, turn the page for a list of my other books. And if you don't want to miss any future releases, please join my newsletter:

http://kayleacross.com/v2/newsletter/

Complete Booklist

ROMANTIC SUSPENSE

Colebrook Siblings Trilogy
Brody's Vow
Wyatt's Stand
Easton's Claim

Hostage Rescue Team Series
Marked
Targeted
Hunted
Disavowed
Avenged
Exposed
Seized
Wanted
Betrayed
Reclaimed

Titanium Security Series
Ignited
Singed
Burned
Extinguished
Rekindled
Blindsided: A Titanium Christmas Novella

Bagram Special Ops Series
Deadly Descent
Tactical Strike
Lethal Pursuit
Danger Close

Collateral Damage
Never Surrender (a MacKenzie Family novella)

Suspense Series
Out of Her League
Cover of Darkness
No Turning Back
Relentless
Absolution

PARANORMAL ROMANCE
Empowered Series
Darkest Caress

HISTORICAL ROMANCE
The Vacant Chair

EROTIC ROMANCE (writing as *Callie Croix*)
Deacon's Touch
Dillon's Claim
No Holds Barred
Touch Me
Let Me In
Covert Seduction

Acknowledgements

Thanks to my readers, for inspiring me to write this story. And to my editing and production team, for helping me get this one ready.

About the Author

NY Times and USA Today Bestselling author Kaylea Cross writes edge-of-your-seat military romantic suspense. Her work has won many awards and has been nominated for both the Daphne du Maurier and the National Readers' Choice Awards. A former Registered Massage Therapist by trade, Kaylea is also an avid gardener, artist, Civil War buff, Special Ops aficionado, belly dance enthusiast and former nationally-carded softball pitcher. She lives in Vancouver, BC with her husband and family.

You can visit Kaylea at www.kayleacross.com. If you would like to be notified of future releases, please join her newsletter:

http://kayleacross.com/v2/newsletter/

CPSIA information can be obtained
at www.ICGtesting.com
Printed in the USA
LVHW111630230721
693425LV00016B/1249